"Do you like to laugh?" Joe asked.

"Sure."

"And do you enjoy making other people laugh?"

She shrugged. "I suppose so."

"Then maybe you've got what it takes to be a clown." Joe grinned. "Don't mind me—I'm always trying to recruit others to become clowns."

Lois wasn't sure what to say in response, so she merely turned her head away and stared out the window. The idea of her becoming a clown seemed ridiculous. She studied her little green car sitting under the street light. If she could only come up with a legitimate excuse, she'd forget about her chocolate treat and head straight for home. Joe Richey was cute and funny, but at the moment he was making her feel rather uncomfortable.

WANDA E. BRUNSTETTER lives in Central Washington with her husband who is a pastor. She has two grown children and six grandchildren. Her hobbies include doll repairing, sewing, ventriloquism, stamping, reading, and gardening. Wanda and her husband have a puppet ministry, which they often share at other churches, Bible camps, and Bible schools. Wanda invites you to visit her website: http://hometown.aol.com/rlbweb/index.html

Books by Wanda E. Brunstetter

HEARTSONG PRESENTS
HP254—A Merry Heart
HP421—Looking for a Miracle
HP465—Talking for Two
HP478—Plain and Fancy
HP486—The Hope Chest
HP517—The Neighborly Thing To Do

Don't miss out on any of our super romances. Write to us at the following address for information on our newest releases and club information.

Heartsong Presents Readers' Service
PO Box 719
Uhrichsville, OH 44683

Or visit www.heartsongpresents.com

Clowning Around

Wanda E. Brunstetter

Heartsong Presents

To Gordon, Kathy, Dell, and Bev—special friends who are great at clowning around.

A note from the Author:
I love to hear from my readers! You may correspond with me by writing:

Wanda E. Brunstetter
Author Relations
PO Box 719
Uhrichsville, OH 44683

ISBN 1-58660-770-7

CLOWNING AROUND

PRINTED IN THE U.S.A.

one

Lois Johnson slid her fingers across the polished surface of her desktop. *I love this job,* she told herself with a smile. She had been working as secretary for Bayview Christian Church only a few weeks, but she already felt at ease. She wasn't making as much money now, she reminded herself, but she had a lot less pressure than when she'd worked as a legal secretary in downtown Tacoma.

Lois hoped her job here would be a ministry, so she could do something meaningful while using her secretarial skills. She was a fairly new Christian, having accepted the Lord as her personal Savior during a recent evangelistic crusade. Now she had an opportunity to work in her home church where she felt comfortable.

Her older sister, Tabby, had told her about the position. Tabby worked in the daycare center sponsored by Bayview Church and had heard that Mildred Thompson, the secretary then, was moving to California. Tabby had notified Lois right away, knowing she wasn't happy in her old job.

A vision of Tabby and her husband, Seth Beyers, performing their ventriloquist routine flashed into Lois's mind. The young couple worked well together, shared a love for Christ and the church, and were so much in love.

Lois stared at the blank computer screen in front of her then pushed the button to turn it on. *I hope I can find an area of service as Tabby and Seth have.* After attending the church for a year, she had signed up to teach a first-grade Sunday school class. She enjoyed working with children and felt she was helping to mold their young lives in some small way. But she wondered if she could be doing more.

As Lois waited for the computer to boot up, she let her mind wander. She'd come a long way in the last few months. The pain of breaking up with her ex-fiancé had diminished considerably. Since she'd become a Christian and started reading her Bible every day and spending time in prayer, her attitude toward many things had changed. No longer was she consumed with a desire for wealth and prestige. She knew money in itself wasn't a bad thing, but her yearning for more, simply for personal gain, had been wrong. Instead of being so self-centered and harsh—especially with her sister, who had been shy and had suffered with a problem of stuttering—with God's help, Lois was learning to be more patient and kind.

Thank You, Lord, for helping Tabby overcome her problems and for changing my heart. Show me the best way to serve You. She hesitated. *And if You have a man out there for me, please let me know he's the right one.*

Lois frowned and twirled her finger around a long, blond curl. She'd been wounded deeply when Michael Yehley postponed their wedding. Then he broke things off completely once she started inviting him to go with her to church. He'd made it clear he had no interest in religious things, didn't need them, and could take care of himself.

Lois knew Michael hadn't been right for her. She also knew she could never love another man who wasn't a Christian or whose only goal in life was climbing the ladder of success. *Lord, if You have a man in mind for me, then he'll have to fall into my lap because I'm not planning to look for anyone. The chances of that are slim to none,* Lois told herself.

⁊

Joe Richey was exhausted. He'd been on the road six weeks, doing a series of family crusades, Bible schools, and church camp meetings. He'd even managed to squeeze in a couple of kids' birthday parties. As much as he enjoyed clowning, he needed to rest. He'd just finished a five-day Bible school in Aberdeen, Washington, which had ended this morning at eleven o'clock. On his way home, he had stopped at the cemetery to visit his parents' graves. When Joe was eight years old, his father was killed in an accident involving the tour bus he drove around the Pacific Northwest. His mother had passed away last summer from lung cancer.

A knot formed in Joe's stomach when he opened the front door of his modest, two-story home in Olympia. When his mother died, he hadn't shed a single tear, and he wasn't about to cry now. In fact, Joe hadn't cried since his father's death almost seventeen years ago. If today hadn't been the anniversary of his mother's death, he probably wouldn't have stopped at the cemetery. It was a painful reminder of his past.

Carrying his red-and-green-checkered clown costume in one hand and a battered suitcase in the other, Joe trudged up the steps to the second floor. He entered his bedroom and flung open the closet door. "Maybe I should take off for a few days and head to the beach," he said aloud, setting the suitcase on the floor and hanging up his costume. "But right now, I guess I'll settle for a hot bath and a long nap."

He yanked a red, rubber clown nose out of his shirt pocket and stuffed it into the drawer where all his clown makeup and props were kept. "I'll be okay. Just need to keep a stiff upper lip and a smile plastered on my face." Joe glanced in the mirror attached to his closet door and forced his mouth to curve upward.

The phone rang sharply. He crossed the room and lifted the receiver from the nightstand by his bed. "Joe Richey here."

He listened to the woman on the other end of the line, nodding occasionally and writing the information she gave him on a notepad. "Uh-huh. Sure. My schedule's been as tight as a jar of pickles all summer, but things are slowing down some now. I'm sure I can work it in. Okay, thanks."

Joe hung up the phone and sank onto the bed with a moan. "One more crusade, and then I'll take a little vacation." He glanced over the notes he'd jotted down. "It's only a forty-five-minute drive from Olympia to Tacoma. It'll be a piece of cake."

❧

After discussing the church bulletin with Richard Smith, the associate pastor, Lois returned to her desk, and the phone rang. She smiled when she heard her sister's voice. "Hi, Tabby, what's up?"

"I was wondering if you could meet me for lunch today."

"Sure—sounds good. Should I come downstairs to the day care, or do you want to come up here?"

"Neither. I'd like to take you out for lunch. You've been cooped up in that office so much since you started working here, even eating lunch at your desk sometimes. Today's Friday, so I think we should celebrate. Let's go to Garrison's Deli."

Lois sighed. She didn't feel much like going out, even though the sun was shining brightly on this pleasant summer day and the fresh air would probably do her some good. She preferred to stay at her desk and eat the bag lunch she'd brought, but she didn't want to disappoint Tabby. She'd done plenty of that in the past. Now that Lois was trying to live her faith, she made every attempt to please rather than tease her sister.

"Sure—what time?" Lois asked.

"Donna's taking her lunch break at noon, so how does one o'clock sound?"

"Great. See you then." Lois hung up the phone and grabbed that day's mail. The first letter contained a flyer announcing a special service at another church in the north end of Tacoma. It listed all the people in the program, including Tabby and Seth. Lois noticed the program was a little over a week away, so she decided to make copies of the flyer and insert one into each bulletin to be handed out on Sunday.

By twelve-thirty, Lois had finished the bulletins and was stuffing the flyers inside each one when Sam Hanson, the senior pastor, stepped into her office. "Have you had lunch yet, Lois?" he asked. Sam and his wife Norma were always concerned about her.

She shook her head but kept her eyes focused on the work she was doing. "I'm meeting Tabby at Garrison's Deli in half an hour."

"That's good to hear. I was afraid you planned to work through lunch again."

Lois looked up. "Not today."

The pastor smiled. "I'm glad you're taking your position seriously, Lois, but we don't want you to work too hard."

"I'm grateful for the opportunity to work here." Lois smiled too. "I love my new job, and sometimes it's hard to tear myself away."

"Which is precisely why Norma and I think you should get out more," he said. "A lovely young woman like you needs an active social life."

She shrugged. "I do get out. I drive to Olympia to visit my folks at least twice a month."

"That's not quite what we meant."

"I know, but I'm okay, really."

Pastor Hanson nodded. "Anytime you need to talk, though, I'm a good listener. And so is Norma." He winked. "Since my office is right next door, you won't have far to go."

"Thanks, Pastor. I'll keep that in mind."

৯

Lois found Tabby waiting in a booth at the deli. "Sorry I'm a few minutes late," she said, dropping into the seat across from her sister.

Tabby smiled, her dark eyes gleaming. "No problem. I figured you probably had an important phone call or something. I've only been here a few minutes, but I took the liberty of ordering us each a veggie sandwich on whole wheat bread, with cream cheese and lots of alfalfa sprouts."

Lois chuckled. "We may not look much like sisters, but we sure have the same taste in food." She nodded toward the counter. "What did you order us to drink?"

"Strawberry lemonade for you and an iced tea with a slice of lemon for me."

"Umm. Sounds good. An ice-cold lemonade on a hot day like this should hit the spot."

"It is pretty warm," Tabby agreed. "Kind of unusual weather for Tacoma, even if it is still summer."

"I heard on the news that it might reach ninety by the weekend," Lois commented.

Tabby's dark eyebrows raised. "Guess we'd better find a way to cool off then."

Lois drew in a breath. Last year she'd been invited to use

the Yehleys' swimming pool on several occasions. It was heated, so even when the weather was cool, the pool was a great place to exercise or simply relax. Lois wouldn't be swimming in Michael's pool this year, though. She didn't care. She could always go to one of the many fitness centers in town or, if she felt brave, take a dip in the chilly waters of Puget Sound Bay. Michael and his parents had no place in her life anymore, and neither did their pool!

"Lois. Earth to Lois."

Lois's eyelids fluttered. "Oh—you were talking to me, and I was daydreaming?"

Tabby laughed. "Something like that."

"What were you saying?"

"I was telling you about the special service Westside Community Church is having a week from Saturday night."

Lois nodded. "I already know. We received a flyer in the mail today."

Tabby frowned. "Kind of late notice, wouldn't you say?"

"That's what I thought, but I made copies and inserted them in the bulletins for this Sunday."

"Seth and I are doing a ventriloquist routine," Tabby said.

"Yes, I saw your names on the flyer."

They heard their order being announced, and Tabby slid out of the booth. "I'll be right back."

"Want some help?" Lois called after her.

"No, thanks. I can manage."

When Tabby returned a few minutes later, Lois offered up a prayer, and they started eating their sandwiches.

"I was hoping you would come to the service at Westside," Tabby said between bites. "You don't go out much anymore, and I thought—"

Lois held up her hand. "You thought you'd apply a little pressure." She clucked her tongue against the roof of her mouth. "You and the Hansons wouldn't be in cahoots, would you?"

Tabby flicked her shoulder-length, chestnut-colored hair away from her face. "Whatever gave you such a notion?"

Lois lifted her gaze toward the ceiling. "I can't imagine."

"I really would like you to come," Tabby said. "Seth and I will do our routine, they'll have a gospel clown and an illusionist, and Donna's going to do one of her beautiful chalk art drawings." She leaned across the table and studied Lois intently. "If it weren't for a creative illusionist's testimony, you probably wouldn't be where you are today."

Lois narrowed her eyes. "You mean sitting here at Garrison's, drinking strawberry lemonade, and eating a delicious sandwich?"

Tabby grinned. "I meant that you wouldn't be working for our church. For that matter, if you hadn't committed your life to Christ during a crusade, you probably wouldn't be going to church."

"I know."

"So will you come to the program? I always feel better when I look out into the audience and see your beautiful face smiling back at me."

Lois grinned. How could she say no to the most wonderful sister in the world? "I'll be there—right in the front row."

two

Joe stood in the small room near the main platform in the sanctuary of Westside Community Church, waiting his turn. He was dressed in a pair of baggy blue jeans, with a matching jacket, decorated with multicolored patches. He wore a bright orange shirt under his jacket, a polka-dot tie, and a bright-red rubber nose. Attached to his hair was a red yarn wig, and a floppy blue hat perched on top. Black oversized shoes turning up at the toes completed his clown costume.

Joe peeked through the stage door window and saw Seth and Tabby Beyers on stage with their two dummies. He had watched the young couple perform on other programs and knew audiences loved them. Their unusual ventriloquist routine would be hard to follow.

I'm not doing this merely to entertain, Joe reminded himself. *It isn't important whom the audience likes best. What counts is whether we get across the message of salvation and Christian living.* Entertain, but have a positive impact on people's lives—that's what he'd been taught at the gospel clowning school where he'd received his training several years ago.

Joe reached inside the pocket of his clown suit, and his fingers curled around a stash of balloons. He knew one of the best things in his routine was the balloons he twisted into various animals. After every performance, a group of excited kids would surround him, wanting to talk to the goofy clown and to get a balloon animal.

13

Joe heard his name being called and grabbed the multi-colored duffel bag that held his props. For some reason he felt edgy tonight. He didn't understand it because he had done hundreds of programs like this one. He figured it must be due to fatigue since he'd been on the road so much lately and needed a vacation.

Then "Slow-Joe the Clown" stepped onto the stage. Opening his bag of tricks, he withdrew a huge plastic hammer with a shackle attached. He held the mallet over his head. "I'm all set now to open my own hamburger chain," he announced.

The audience laughed, and Joe moved to the edge of the platform, holding his props toward the spectators. "If my hamburger chain doesn't work out, I'm thinking about raising rabbits." He pursed his lips. "Of course, I'm gonna have to keep 'em indoors, so they'll be ingrown hares."

Everyone laughed again, and Joe winked, dropped the hammer back into the bag, and pulled out a blue balloon. He blew into it, holding the end and stretching the latex as the balloon inflated. Tying a knot, he twisted two small bubbles in the center of the balloon and locked them together in one quick twist. Then he made five bubbles and formed the body of a baby seal. The lowest part of the balloon was the neck, and Joe added another bubble at the top, so the seal looked as if it were balancing a ball on the end of its nose.

Gripping his floppy hat, Joe tipped his head back and balanced the balloon seal on the end of his rubber nose. The crowd roared as he moved slowly about the stage, waving one hand and trying to keep the seal in place. When the seal toppled off, Joe explained how some people try to balance their lives between church, home, and extracurricular activities but don't always succeed.

Then he twisted more balloons into a blue whale, a hump-back camel, and a lion with a mane. After each creation, Joe told a Bible story, including one about Daniel in the lions' den.

Next, Joe grabbed five red balls from his bag, tossing them one at a time into the air and juggling them. As he did so, he faced the audience. "I often get busy with my clowning schedule and have to juggle my time a bit. But I always feel closer to God when I take time out to read the Bible and pray. Just like juggling balls, our lives can get crazy and out of line with God's will."

Joe let one ball drop to the floor. "I took my eyes off the ball and messed up." He caught the other four balls in his hands and bent down to pick up the one he'd dropped. "The nice thing about juggling is, I can always start over again whenever I've made a mistake. The same is true of my spiritual life. God is always there, waiting for me to trust Him and accept His love and forgiveness for me."

Joe concluded his routine by creating a vibrant balloon bouquet that resembled a bunch of tulips. "I'd like to recognize someone special in the audience," he said, shading his eyes with his hand and staring out at the congregation. "Nope. I don't recognize a soul!"

Several people chuckled. Then he asked, "Has anyone recently had a birthday?"

Murmurs drifted through the crowd, but no one spoke up.

"Okay—let's do this another way. Anyone have a birthday today?" Silence greeted him. He waved the bouquet in the air. "How about last week?" Still no response. "Come now, folks—don't be shy. I'm sure at least one person in this group has had a birthday recently."

At last someone's hand went up in the front row. Joe

grinned. "Ah-ha—a pretty lady with long blond hair has finally responded."

તે

Lois slid down in her seat. *What in the world possessed me to raise my hand?* She'd celebrated her twenty-second birthday two weeks ago, but she didn't need the whole audience looking at her now, which was exactly what they were doing!

The tall clown moved toward her. He wore a broad smile on his white-painted face, and his hand was outstretched. "A beautiful bouquet for the birthday gal," he said with a deep chuckle.

Lois forced herself to smile in return.

"Do you know what flowers grow between your nose and chin?"

She shook her head.

"Tulips!"

Everyone laughed, and the clown winked at Lois. "Would you like to tell us your name and when you celebrated your birthday?"

"My name is Lois Johnson, and my birthday was two weeks ago."

Slow-Joe shuffled his feet, lifted his floppy hat, then plopped it back down on his head. "Ta-da!" He held out the bouquet to her.

Suddenly, the young girl sitting beside Lois bounced up and down, crying, "I want a balloon! I want a balloon!" She leaped out of her seat and lunged forward, obviously hoping to grab a balloon out of Slow-Joe's hands. Instead she tripped and tumbled against his knees. He wobbled back and forth, and the audience laughed loudly.

Lois wondered if this were part of the act, but suddenly Joe fell forward and landed in her lap. She figured it had to be an accident and the child was just over-excited. Or was it? Hadn't she told God that if He wanted her to have a man, He'd have to drop him into her lap? She swallowed hard and stared into the clown's hazel eyes.

"Sorry," he mumbled. "Don't know how that happened." He handed Lois the balloon bouquet and stood up. He turned back to face the audience and wiggled his dark eyebrows. "Let's sing the birthday song to Lois, shall we?"

Lois felt the heat of embarrassment creep up her neck. *This is what I get for being dumb enough to raise my hand.*

The young girl who had been sitting next to her now stood beside the clown. Before anyone could say anything, she started singing at the top of her lungs: "Happy Birthday to you. . ."

The audience joined in, and Lois stared straight ahead, wishing she could make herself invisible. When the song was over, she leaned toward Slow-Joe and whispered, "Thanks for the flowers."

He nodded, took a bow, and dashed backstage.

Lois sat through the rest of the program feeling as if she were in a daze. Why had the clown singled her out? *Well, after all, I did raise my hand when he asked who'd had a birthday recently,* she reminded herself. *What else could he do?*

When the service was over, Lois made her way to the foyer, where she found Tabby and Seth standing by the front door. She tapped her sister on her shoulder. "You guys were great as usual."

Tabby turned and smiled. "Thanks. Your part of the program wasn't bad either."

"Yeah, we were watching from off-stage," Seth said, patting

Lois on the back. "Maybe you should leave your secretarial job and become a clown. You had the audience in stitches."

Lois groaned. "It was that goofy clown who made everyone laugh." She shook her head. "It was bad enough that he fell into my lap, but he only embarrassed me more by having everyone sing to me."

"Aw, it was all in fun," Seth said with a chuckle.

"We're heading out for some pie and coffee. Want to join us?" Tabby asked, giving Lois a little nudge.

She shrugged. "Sure—why not? At least there I won't have any reason to hide my face."

three

The all-night coffee shop Seth picked was bustling with activity. Lois slipped into a booth by the window, and Tabby and Seth took the other side.

"You ladies feel free to order anything you want," Seth said, offering Lois a wide smile. "This is my treat, so you may as well go overboard and order something really fattening if you feel so inclined."

Tabby snickered. "Does my little sister look as if she ever goes overboard when it comes to eating?" She wagged a finger toward Lois. "What I wouldn't give to have a figure like yours."

Lois shook her head. "My high metabolism and a half hour of aerobics every day might help keep me looking thin, but I have been known to indulge. Especially when chocolate is involved."

"Women and their addiction to chocolate!" Seth grabbed Tabby's hand and gave it a squeeze. "I guess if that's your worst sin, I can consider myself very blessed."

Tabby groaned. "You know I'm far from perfect, Seth."

"What's this about someone being perfect?"

The three young people turned toward the masculine voice. Even without his costume and clown makeup, Lois would have recognized that smile. Slow-Joe the Clown wiggled his eyebrows and gave her a crooked grin.

"Good to see you, Joe. I was just telling my beautiful wife

how lucky I am to have her." Seth gestured toward the empty seat next to Lois. "Why don't you take a load off those big clown feet and join us for pie and coffee?"

"Don't mind if I do." Joe dropped down beside Lois. She squirmed uneasily and slid along the bench until her hip bumped the wall. "It's good to see you again, Birthday Girl." He extended his hand. "I don't think we've been formally introduced. I'm Joe Richey."

"I—I'm Lois Johnson," she said. "Tabby's my sister, and Seth is my brother-in-law."

As they shook hands, Joe's face broke into a broad smile. "Sure hope I didn't embarrass you too much during my performance tonight."

"Well—"

"So tell me, Seth—how'd you meet this perfect wife of yours?" Joe asked, changing the subject abruptly.

Lois felt a sense of irritation, but at the same time she was relieved Joe had interrupted her and taken the conversation in another direction. At least she wasn't the focus of their discussion anymore.

"Tabby took one of my ventriloquist classes, and I was drawn to her like a moth heading straight for a flame." Seth turned his head and gave Tabby a noisy kiss on her cheek.

Joe chuckled. "Since I'm not married, I don't consider myself an expert on the subject, but I recently heard about a man who met his wife at a travel bureau."

"Oh?" Seth said with obvious interest. "And what's so unusual about that?"

Joe grinned and turned to wink at Lois. "She was looking for a vacation, and he was the last resort."

Everyone laughed, and Lois felt herself begin to relax.

"Adam and Eve had the only perfect marriage," Joe continued, his eyes looking suddenly serious.

"What makes you say that?" asked Tabby.

Joe tapped his knuckles on the table. "Think about it. Adam didn't have to hear about all the men Eve could have married, and Eve wasn't forced to listen to a bunch of stories about the way Adam's mother cooked."

Seth howled, and Tabby slapped him playfully on the arm. He tickled her under the chin. "The other day I heard my wife telling our neighbors I was a model husband. I felt pretty good about that until I looked up the word in a dictionary."

"What did it say?" Lois asked, putting her elbows on the table and leaning forward.

"A model is a small imitation of the real thing."

Another gale of laughter went around the table, but the waitress came then to take their order. Lois figured it was time to get serious, so she ordered a cup of herbal tea and a brownie. Tabby settled for coffee and a maple bar. Both men asked for coffee and hot-apple pie, topped with vanilla ice cream. While they waited for their orders, the joke-telling continued.

"I've heard that marriage is comparable to twirling a baton, turning hand springs, or eating with chopsticks," Joe said with a sly grin on his face. "It looks really easy 'til you try it."

"I wouldn't know. I'm an old maid of twenty-two," Lois interjected.

Joe bobbed his head up and down and chuckled. "Wow, that is pretty old."

Tabby wrinkled her nose. "Not to be outdone—when Seth and I got married, it was for better or worse. I couldn't do better, and he couldn't do worse."

Remembering the days of her sister's low self-esteem, Lois quickly jumped in. "That's not true, Tabby, and you know it."

Tabby raised her eyebrows and looked at Lois. "I was only kidding."

Joe nudged Lois gently in the ribs with his elbow. "Did you know this is National Clown Month?"

She shook her head.

"Yes, and as a clown I feel it's my duty to make as many people laugh as possible." Joe then tapped Lois on the shoulder. "Do you like to laugh?"

"Sure."

"And do you enjoy making other people laugh?"

She shrugged. "I suppose so."

"Then maybe you've got what it takes to be a clown." Joe grinned. "Don't mind me—I'm always trying to recruit others to become clowns."

Lois wasn't sure what to say in response, so she merely turned her head away and stared out the window. The idea of her becoming a clown seemed ridiculous. She studied her little green car sitting under the street light next to Seth's black Bronco. If she could only come up with a legitimate excuse, she'd forget about her chocolate treat and head straight for home. Joe Richey was cute and funny, but at the moment he was making her feel rather uncomfortable.

❧

Joe clenched his teeth and squished the napkin in his lap into a tight ball. *I think I've blown it with this woman. I had her laughing one minute, and the next minute she's giving me the silent treatment. What'd I say or do that turned her off?*

"When will your next performance be, Joe?" Seth asked.

"Tonight was my last one for awhile."

"How come?" Tabby questioned. "I'd think a funny guy like you would be in high demand."

"I guess I am, because I've been doing back-to-back programs all summer," Joe said. "I'm in need of a break, though. Thought I might head for the beach or go up to Mt. Rainier to relax."

Seth nodded. "Makes sense to me. All work and no play— well, you know the rest of that saying. Even Jesus needed to get away from the crowds once in awhile. If you don't take time for yourself, you'll burn out like a candle in the wind."

"How long have you been clowning?" Lois asked.

At least she's speaking to me again. Joe turned his head and offered her his best smile. "Ever since I was a kid, but professionally for about two years."

As Joe leaned even closer to Lois, his senses were assaulted by the subtle fragrance of peaches. *It must be her shampoo.* He wondered if her hair was as soft as it looked, and he fought the urge to reach out and touch the long, golden tresses. "Do you live around here, Lois?" he asked.

"Tabby and I grew up in Olympia, and our folks still live there." Lois smiled. "We both settled in Tacoma when we found jobs here."

Joe tapped the edge of his water glass with one finger. "I'm from Olympia too."

"Really? What part of town?" Lois asked.

"The north side."

"Lois drives to Olympia a couple of times a month," Tabby said, smiling at Joe. "Maybe you two should get together sometime."

❧

Lois nearly choked on the sip of water she'd just taken. She had the distinct feeling she was being set up. Maybe her well-meaning sister had planned it so Joe would meet them at the coffee shop. It might be that the little schemer was trying to play matchmaker. *Who knows? Tabby could have been behind that whole scenario at the church tonight. She may have asked Joe to single me out with the balloon bouquet and birthday song.*

Lois resolved to have a little heart-to-heart talk with her sister. If she ever had another man in her life, she needed to do the picking. Tabby might have her best interests at heart, but she wasn't Lois's keeper. Besides, Lois wasn't looking for a man now.

She gave Joe a sidelong glance, and he smiled, a slow, lazy grin that set her heart racing. *He sure is cute. And he did fall into my lap.* The waitress brought their desserts, which helped Lois force her thoughts off the man who was sitting much too close. She concentrated on the piece of chocolate decadence on her plate. A little sugar for her sweet tooth and some herbal tea to soothe her nerves, and she would be right as rain.

four

"Don't keep me in suspense. Did he call or what?"

Lois glanced over her shoulder. Tabby had just entered the church office and was looking at her like an expectant child waiting to open her birthday presents.

"Did who call?"

"Joe Richey."

"No, he didn't call," Lois answered as she shut down her computer for the day.

"You did give him your phone number, didn't you? I thought I saw you hand him a slip of paper the other night when we were at the coffee shop."

Lois slid her chair away from the desk and stood up. "Tabby Beyers, get a life!"

Tabby folded her arms across her chest and wrinkled her nose. "I have a life. I'm a wife, a daycare worker, and a ventriloquist."

Lois puckered her lips. "Then that ought to keep you busy enough so you can manage to mind your own business and not mine."

Tabby stuck out her tongue. "For your information, I'm only interested in your welfare."

"I appreciate that." Lois smiled, her irritation lessening. "If you don't mind, though, I think I can worry about my own welfare."

Tabby shrugged. "Whatever you say. Starting next month I won't be around much to meddle in your life, anyway."

Lois drew her brows together. "What's that supposed to mean? You and Seth aren't planning to move, I hope."

Tabby shook her head. "We'd never intentionally move from Tacoma. We like it here too much." She fluttered her lashes. "It's all that liquid sunshine, you know."

Lois laughed and reached for her purse, hanging on the coat tree by the door. "If you're not moving, then why won't you be around much?"

"We're going on an evangelistic tour with several other Christian workers," Tabby explained. "We'll be traveling around the state of Washington and to a few places in Oregon and Idaho. Probably be gone at least a month. Maybe longer if we get a good response."

"Is Slow-Joe the Clown going with you?" Lois asked. She didn't know why, but she hoped he wasn't. They'd only met a few nights ago, so she hardly knew the man. She'd never admit it to Tabby, but Joe had promised to call. She looked forward to it, because there was something about the goofy guy that stirred her interest, even if she had felt uncomfortable in his presence. She wasn't sure if it were his silly antics and wisecracks, his hazel eyes with the gold flecks, or his mop of curly brown hair that made him so appealing.

"Lois, are you listening to me?"

Lois whirled around to face her sister. "Huh?"

"You asked if Joe Richey was going on tour with us, and I said no. But you're standing there staring at your purse as if you're in a world of your own." Tabby wrinkled her nose. "I'm sure you didn't hear a word I said."

Lois laughed self-consciously. "I guess I was kind of in my own world."

Tabby's eyes narrowed. "Thinking about Joe, I'll bet."

Lois couldn't deny it, so she asked another question. "If you're going on tour for a month or longer, how will Donna manage the day care?"

Tabby waved her hand. "She already has that covered. Corrie, our helper, has a friend who has been taking some child development classes. Donna thought she'd give her a try." She shrugged. "Who knows? Maybe I'll quit the day care. Then Corrie can take my place."

"Quit the day care?" Lois could hardly believe it. "But you love working with the kids. I can't imagine your doing anything else."

Tabby started for the door. "How about becoming a full-time mother?"

Lois's mouth dropped open. "You're pregnant?"

"Not yet, but I'm hopeful. Seth and I have been married two years, you know. We both think it's time to start a family."

Sudden envy surged through Lois, and she blinked several times to hold back tears that threatened to spill over. She loved children. That was why she was teaching a Sunday school class. How ironic. *Tabby used to be jealous of me, and now I feel the same way toward her. Help me in this area, Lord.*

৯

Joe searched through his closet for the right clothes to take to the beach. It could be windy, cold, rainy, or sunny along the Washington coast, even during the month of August. He'd probably need to take a couple of sweatshirts, some shorts, one or two pairs of jeans and, of course, his most comfortable pair of sneakers.

His favorite thing to do at the ocean was beachcomb. The flower beds in his backyard gave evidence of that. Pieces of driftwood adorned nearly every bed, and scattered throughout the plants were shells of all sizes and shapes. Stationed beside his front door were two buoys he'd discovered after a winter storm one year, and a fishbowl full of beach agates was displayed on his fireplace mantel.

Joe wondered why he didn't sell the old house he'd grown up in and buy a small cabin near the beach. He knew it would be more peaceful there. But then he'd be farther from the cities where he found most of his work.

As he packed his clothes into his suitcase, Joe noticed one of his clown suits lying on the floor. He'd forgotten to put it in the hamper.

Joseph Andrew Richey, you're a slob! You need to learn to pick up after yourself. Joe could hear his mother's sharp words, as if she were standing right there in his room.

She had always been a neat freak, unless she was in one of her down moods. Then she didn't care what she or the house looked like. Joe could never understand how his mother could yell at her children one day to pick up their things and the next day sink into such despair that she'd need a bulldozer to clear the clutter off the kitchen table.

"No wonder Brian left home the day he turned eighteen," Joe mumbled. He bent down to pick up the clown suit and shook his head. "I wouldn't be surprised if my little brother isn't still running from job to job, trying to dodge his problems."

His brother had a hot temper and had been fired from several positions because he couldn't work well with others and didn't want to take orders from his boss. Joe prayed for Brian regularly, but he'd given up trying to talk to him; their last discussion had ended in a horrible argument, and Joe figured he might never hear from his brother again.

Pushing thoughts of his brother aside, Joe dropped the clown suit into the hamper. Without warning, another one of his mother's accusations pounded in his head.

You're not going to wash that without checking the pockets, I hope.

Joe chuckled. "No, Mom. I wouldn't dream of it."

He stuffed his hand inside one deep pocket and withdrew three red pencil balloons and one green apple balloon. "Whew! Wouldn't want to put these babies in the washing machine."

Joe plunged his hand into the other pocket and pulled out a slip of paper. "Hmm—what's this? Somebody's phone number?" He sank to the edge of his bed and stared at the paper. Who'd recently given him a number, and why hadn't he been smart enough to jot down a name to go with it?

Joe grimaced. He'd probably forget his own name if it weren't on his driver's license.

"Think hard, Joe. Whose number is on this piece of paper?"

Lord, if this phone number is important, help me remember.

Still nothing.

Joe stretched out across the bed, and within a matter of minutes he was asleep. Several hours later he awoke, feeling more refreshed than he had all day.

Sitting up, he noticed the slip of paper lying on the bed. He looked intently at the phone number, and a wide grin spread across his face. "Lois Johnson! Tabby's sister gave me her number when we met at the coffee shop the other night."

Feeling as if he'd been handed an Oscar, Joe grabbed the telephone off the small table by his bed. He punched in the numbers and waited for Lois to pick up, but only a recorded message answered. He hated talking to machines so he didn't leave a message.

"Guess there's no hurry," he assured himself. "I'll call her after I get back from the beach."

five

Joe set his suitcase inside the front door, plodded to the living room, and sank wearily to the couch. Two weeks at the beach should have revived him. But they hadn't. His body felt rested, but he had a sense of unrest deep within his soul. Maybe he would feel better once he started working again. That's what he needed—a few more crusades or a couple of birthday parties to get him back on his feet.

Joe forced himself off the couch and headed for the kitchen. He hoped to find at least one job opportunity waiting for him on his answering machine. He didn't want to start hunting for programs. He had never been good at promoting himself, and so far he hadn't needed to. Word of mouth had served him well.

Among the messages, he heard five requests for his clown routine. Two were for church rallies, and the other three involved birthday parties. Even though the parties were mainly for entertainment, he still felt as if he were doing something worthwhile by providing children with good, clean fun. He usually gave some kind of moral lesson with his balloon animals, so at least the children were being exposed to admirable virtues and not merely being entertained.

Feeling a surge of energy, Joe returned the calls, lined up each program, and wrote the dates and times on his appointment calendar. The business end of Joe's clowning was important, and he tried to stay organized with his programs, even if he weren't always structured at home. It wouldn't do to forget or arrive late for an engagement. In fact, it could cost him jobs if he did it too often.

He was heading upstairs to unpack his suitcase when he spotted the slip of paper with Lois Johnson's number on it. He dialed but reached her answering machine, as he had two weeks ago.

"Isn't that woman ever at home?" Joe muttered. He hung up the phone without leaving a message. "I'll try again after I unpack and see if there's anything in the refrigerator to eat."

❧

Pastor Hanson had insisted Lois take off early from work today so she decided to explore some of the new stores at the Tacoma Mall. She didn't have a lot of money to spend, but she knew how to shop for bargains. If a store were having a good deal on something, she'd be sure to find it. Besides, Tabby and Seth had left the day before, and she was feeling lonely. A little shopping would help take her mind off her troubles. At least it would be a temporary diversion.

Lois parked her car in the lot on the north side of the mall then slipped off her navy blue pumps and replaced them with a pair of comfortable walking shoes. It might not look fashionable to shop in an ankle-length navy-blue dress and a pair of black sneakers, but she didn't care. It wasn't likely she'd see anyone she knew at the mall.

Lois grabbed her purse, hopped out of the car, and jogged to the mall's closest entrance. Her first stop was a women's clothing store where she found two blouses for under ten dollars and a pair of shorts that had been marked down to five dollars because summer was nearly over.

Next she entered a bed and bath store in hopes of finding a

new shower curtain. Her old one had water stains and was beginning to tear. The clerk showed her several, but they cost too much. Lois was about to give up when she noticed a man heading her way. She stood frozen in her tracks, her body trembling.

Lois glanced around for something to hide behind, but it was too late. Michael Yehley was striding toward her, an arrogant smile on his face. Feelings of the old hurt and humiliation knifed through her, and she fought to keep from dashing out of the store.

"Well, well, if it isn't my beautiful ex-fiancée," Michael drawled. He was dressed in a dark brown business suit, white shirt, and olive-green tie with tan pinstripes. He had never projected a flashy image, but he did carry about him an air of superiority. His dark hair, parted on the side, his aristocratic nose, and his metal-framed glasses gave him a distinguished appearance Lois had once found attractive.

She took a step back as he reached for her hand. "H–hello, Michael. I'm surprised to see you here."

"My mother's birthday is coming up, and I thought I'd get something for her newly redecorated bath." He grinned at her. "She's going with an oriental theme this time."

This time? How many other times has your mother redecorated her bathroom? Lois feigned a smile. "I'm sure she'll like whatever you choose. You always did have impeccable taste."

Michael looked directly at her. "I thought so when I chose you." He wrinkled his nose, as though some foul odor had suddenly permeated the room. "Of course, that was before you flipped out and went religious on me."

Lois swallowed hard. Michael first postponed their wedding because he thought she was too young and they hadn't known each other long enough. But later, after she became a Christian, he had forced her to choose between him and God. When she told him she wouldn't give up her relationship with Christ, he'd said some choice words and stormed out of her apartment. He had called a few weeks later, informing Lois she was acting like a confused little girl and that she should call if she ever came to her senses. That had been two years ago, but even now it hurt. Especially with Michael looking at her as if she'd been crazy for choosing God over him. She certainly didn't want the man back in her life. She had tried hard enough after her conversion to get him to attend church, but it always caused an argument. Michael had been adamant about not needing any kind of religious crutch, and he'd told her he wasn't going to church, no matter how many times she asked.

"How about joining me for a cup of coffee?" Michael asked. "We can try out that new place on the other side of the mall."

Lois opened her mouth, but he cut her off. "It'll be like old times, and you can fill me in on what you've been up to lately." He gave her a charming smile. "Besides, you look kind of down. Hot coffee and some time with me will surely cheer you up."

Lois shook her head. "You know I don't like coffee, Michael."

"You can have tea, soda, whatever you want." He took hold of Lois's arm and steered her toward the door.

"What about the gift you were planning to buy your mother?" she asked.

"It can wait."

Why was she letting him escort her along the mall corridor? Was she so lonely she'd allow him to lead her away like a sheep being led to slaughter?

When they reached the café, Michael found a table. He ordered a mocha-flavored coffee, and Lois asked for a glass of iced tea.

As they waited for their beverages, Michael leaned across the table and studied Lois intently. "Tell me why you quit working for Thorn and Thorn."

Her eyes narrowed. "News sure travels fast. When did you hear I'd quit?"

His lips curved into a smile. "I'm a lawyer, remember, Sweetie? Ray Thorn and I had some business dealings a few weeks ago, and he filled me in."

"I'm working as a secretary for Bayview Christian Church."

He grimaced. "That must mean you're still on your religious soapbox."

Lois glanced down at her hands, folded in her lap. Her knuckles were white, and she was trembling again. Did Michael think it would help if he brought up her faith?

"I'm not on a religious soapbox," she said with clenched teeth. "I love the Lord, I'm enjoying my new job, and—"

He held up one hand. "And you obviously care more about all that than you do me."

She sucked in her bottom lip. "What we once had is over, Michael. You made it perfectly clear you weren't interested in marrying a religious fanatic. And from a scriptural point of view, I knew it would be wrong for us to get married if you weren't a Christian."

Michael's face grew red, and a vein on the side of his neck began to pulsate. "Are you saying I'm not good enough for you?"

"It's not that. With our religious views being so opposite, it wouldn't have worked out. We would always be arguing."

"As we are now?"

She nodded.

The waitress arrived then, and Lois and Michael sat in silence for awhile, sipping their drinks. Lois wished she hadn't come here with him. Nothing good was resulting from this little meeting.

"I'm sorry things didn't work out for us, Michael," she murmured, "but, as I said before, I could never have married someone who didn't share my belief in God."

The waitress brought the bill and placed it next to Michael's cup. He gulped down the rest of his coffee and stood, knocking the receipt to the floor. "Some things never change, and you're obviously one of them!"

He bent down to pick up the bill. "Nice shoes," he said in a mocking tone, as he pointed to Lois's sneakers. "Real stylish."

Lois blinked back the burning tears threatening to spill over. So much for her afternoon shopping spree making her feel better. Michael had a knack for getting under her skin; he'd made her cry on more than one occasion, even when they were dating and supposed to be in love. Lois still found him physically attractive, but now she was even more convinced that he was not her type.

Michael stalked off, but a few seconds later he returned to the table with a grim expression on his face. "I just want you to know—I harbor no ill feelings toward you. I'm getting on with my life, and apparently you are too."

Lois only nodded. Her throat was too clogged with tears, and she was afraid if she tried to speak she would break down. She didn't love Michael anymore, but seeing him again and hearing the way he talked about her faith made her know for certain she'd done the right thing. Her unshed tears were for the time she'd wasted in a relationship that had gone nowhere. She also ached for Michael, that he would discover the same joy she had in a personal relationship with God. Only then had she found freedom from the pursuit of wealth and power, and she wished the same for him. She thought of the people lost in their sin, refusing to acknowledge they'd done anything wrong and turning their backs on God and the salvation He offered through the shed blood of Christ. She sincerely hoped Michael would choose to receive this gift.

Suddenly Michael leaned close to her ear and whispered, "If you should ever come to your senses, give me a call." With that, he kissed her abruptly on the cheek, turned, and was gone.

Lois was too stunned to move. She could scarcely catch her breath.

❧

A half hour later Lois unlocked the door to her apartment and heard the phone ringing. She raced to grab it before the answering machine picked up. "Hello."

"Lois, is that you?"

"Yes. Who's this?"

"Joe Richey—the goofy gospel clown who fell into your lap a few weeks ago."

Lois's heart pounded, and she drew in a breath to steady her nerves. Since he hadn't called, she'd given up hope that he might.

"You still there, Lois?"

His mellow voice stopped her thoughts. "Yes, I'm here—just a little surprised to hear from you."

"I said I'd call, and you did give me your phone number," Joe reminded her.

"I know, but it's been over two weeks, and—"

"And you gave up on me."

"I—I guess I did."

"I've been to Ocean Shores, taking a much-needed vacation."

"Did you have a good time?"

"It was okay. I did a lot of walking on the beach and slept late every morning." Joe chuckled. "Something I hardly ever do when I'm at home."

Lois twirled the phone cord around her finger, wondering what to say next.

"Listen—the reason I'm calling is, I was wondering if you'd like to go bowling this Friday night."

Lois paused as she tried to absorb what Joe had said.

"You do know how to bowl, don't you?"

"Yes, but not very well."

"Maybe I can give you a few pointers. I've been bowling since I was a kid and have a pretty good hook with my ball."

Lois giggled. In her mind's eye she could picture Joe lining up his ball with the pins, snapping his wrist to the left, then acing a strike on the very first ball.

"So what do you say? Would you like to go bowling?"

"Sure—I'd love to."

six

Lois paced between the living room window and the fireplace. Joe should have been here fifteen minutes ago. Had he encountered a lot of traffic on the freeway between Olympia and Tacoma? Had he forgotten the time he'd agreed to come? Maybe he'd stood her up. No, that wasn't likely. Joe seemed too nice of a guy to do something so mean. He did appear to be a bit irresponsible, though. He'd said he would call her after they met at the coffee shop, but he'd gone on vacation and hadn't phoned until two weeks later.

"Sure hope I'm doing the right thing by going out with Joe," Lois murmured. "He's funny and cute, but not really my type." What exactly was her type? She'd once thought Michael fit the criteria—charming, good-looking, smart, and financially well off. Weren't those the qualities she was looking for in a man?

"That was then, and this is now," Lois said as she checked her appearance in the hall mirror. She had a different set of ideals concerning men now. The most important thing was whether he were a Christian or not, and next came compatibility.

The doorbell rang, and Lois jumped. She peered through the peephole in her apartment door and saw one big hazel-colored eye staring back at her.

"Sorry I'm late," Joe apologized when she opened the door. "You gave me your address the other night, but I forgot where I laid it and spent fifteen minutes trying to locate it." Before she could reply, he pulled a bouquet of pink carnations from behind his back and handed them to her. Their hands touched briefly, and Lois was caught off guard by the feelings that stirred deep within.

"I hope these will make up for my forgetfulness," Joe said with a big smile.

Lois smiled, too, and inhaled the subtle fragrance of the bouquet. "Thanks for these. Carnations are my favorite. Come inside while I put them in water."

Joe followed her into the kitchen, and after she'd filled a vase with water and inserted the flowers, she turned to him and smiled. He was dressed in a black-knit polo shirt and a pair of blue jeans. Nothing fancy, yet she thought he looked adorable. *It must be that crooked grin. Or maybe it's his curly brown hair. I wonder what it would feel like to run my fingers through those curls.* Lois halted her thoughts. She barely knew Joe, and after being hurt by Michael she hoped she was smart enough not to rush into another relationship.

"You look great tonight," Joe said. "In fact, we resemble a pair of matching bookends."

Lois glanced down at her black tank top and blue jeans. "Let's hope we match as well at the bowling alley."

"No big deal if we don't." Joe's eyebrows wiggled up and down. "That'll make it more interesting."

৯

Joe sat on the bench, with his arms crossed and a big smile on his face, watching Lois line up her ball with the pins. Her golden hair, held back with two small barrettes, glistened under the bowling alley lights and made him wish he could touch it and feel its softness. He had no plans of becoming emotionally involved with anyone right now, but something about Lois drew him in a way he'd never experienced with other women. Was it merely her good looks, or did Lois have the kind of sweet spirit he desired in a wife? *Wife? Now where did that thought come from?*

Lois squealed with delight when she knocked down half the pins on her first throw, forcing Joe's thoughts back to the game. "Good job!" he exclaimed, pointing both thumbs up in the air.

She pivoted and smiled at him, revealing two dimples he hadn't noticed before. "Not too bad for an amateur, huh?" She grabbed her ball when it returned to the rack and positioned herself in front of the alley. This time her aim was a bit off, and the ball made it halfway down before it veered to the right and rolled into the gutter.

Lois returned to her seat, looking as if she'd lost her best friend. "That little boy a couple of lanes over bowls better than I do."

Joe patted her on the shoulder. "It's only a game, and you're doing your best."

She shrugged. "My best doesn't seem to be good enough."

"You know what they say about practice."

"I don't bowl often enough to get in much practice."

"Guess we'll have to remedy that."

She tipped her head to one side, and her blue eyes sparkled in the light. "Is that your way of asking me out again?"

He grinned. "Sure—if you're interested in dating a goofy guy like me."

Lois giggled and poked him on the arm. "You did look pretty silly awhile ago when you were trying to bowl with your back to the alley."

He tweaked her nose. "Don't slam the technique. I knocked

four pins down that time."

"Next I suppose you'll try to juggle three bowling balls at the same time."

"I think they might be a bit heavy," he answered with a smile. "I could see about juggling three or four pins though."

She jabbed his arm again. "You would, wouldn't you?"

Joe stood up, retrieved his ball from the return rack then turned back to face Lois. "Hang around me long enough, and you'll be surprised at what I can do."

After bowling three games, they walked over to the snack bar for hamburgers and French fries. Joe ordered a cherry soda and Lois a glass of lemonade before finding an empty booth.

Lois eyed Joe curiously as he poured ketchup on his fries. He looked like a little boy in a man's body, with eyes that twinkled like stars, a mouth turned up, and freckles spattered across the bridge of his nose.

He glanced up then. "A nickel for your thoughts," he said, smiling.

She could feel her cheeks grow warm. "Oh, uh, well, I was just wondering about something."

"What is it?"

"Well, I realized I don't know much about you. I know you're a gospel clown and you live in Olympia, but that's about all."

Joe shrugged. "There's not much to tell."

"What about your family?"

"What about them?"

"Do you have any brothers or sisters?"

"Just a brother who's a few years younger than I am."

"Where do your folks live?" she asked.

Joe stared at the table. "They're both dead."

"Oh, I'm sorry. What happened?"

"I'd rather not talk about it right now, if that's okay," he said, looking down at the table.

"Sure," Lois said, suddenly uncomfortable with the direction their conversation had taken. She hesitated before speaking, hoping she could find a better topic to discuss. "Do you work at any other job besides clowning?"

"I went to trade school right out of high school and learned how to be a mechanic," he answered. "I worked at a garage not far from home for awhile, but after I started clowning, the job turned to part-time; finally I quit altogether."

"You mean you make enough money clowning to support yourself?"

He nodded. "Yes, but I'll never be rich. Besides crusades, Bible camps, and other church-related functions, I do birthday parties for kids of all ages. I've also entertained at some senior centers and have even landed a couple of summer jobs at the Enchanted Village near Seattle."

She nodded. "I know where that is. My dad used to take me there when I was a kid."

"What about your sister? Didn't she go too?"

Lois swallowed hard. How could she tell Joe about her childhood and Tabby's without making him think she was a spoiled brat? The truth was that until she trusted the Lord with her life, she'd been exactly that. "Let's just say Tabby was afraid of most of the rides there, and our dad had no patience with her fears."

Joe shook his head slowly. "She sure doesn't seem afraid of much now. In fact, I've seen her do some routines that would rival anything the big-time ventriloquists have done. And she didn't act one bit nervous either."

"Tabby has come a long way in the past few years. All she needed was to gain some confidence, and now she's using her talents to tell others about the Lord." Lois paused. "In the past we weren't very close. I was often critical of her. Things are much better between us now, and I can honestly say I love my sister to pieces. I owe that to the Lord."

Joe leaned across the table and took Lois's hand. A jolt of electricity shot up her arm. "I'm not trying to change the subject, but I've tried calling you a couple of times during the day, and I always get your answering machine. Do you work or go to school someplace in Tacoma?"

"For the past couple of weeks I've been working as the secretary at Bayview Christian Church in the north end of Tacoma," she said.

"And before that?"

"I was a lawyer's secretary."

Joe whistled and released her hand. "Wow! You must have been making some big bucks! What prompted you to give up such a job and take on a church secretary's position, which I'm sure doesn't pay half as much?"

Lois paused. Should she tell Joe about Michael and their broken engagement? It was part of the reason she'd decided to leave her job. The junior partner at the firm was a friend of Michael's, and Lois knew he kept her ex-fiancé updated on her comings and goings. Michael had said as much when they'd run into each other at the mall the other day.

"You're right," she replied. "My job at the church isn't very lucrative, but it does pay the bills, and I consider it to be a ministry of sorts."

His eyebrows lifted. "How so?"

"Many folks call or drop by the church, needing help with food, clothing, or spiritual matters. I'm not a trained counselor so I always send people with serious problems to one of the pastors, but I do pray for those who have a need."

"How long have you been a Christian?" he asked.

"Almost two years. Tabby and I went to church when we were kids, but I never took it seriously until shortly after she and Seth got married. I think seeing how my sister changed when she started using her talents to tell others about the Lord helped me see the emptiness in my own life." Lois lowered her gaze. "I wasn't a very nice person before I became a Christian. The truth is I was spoiled and self-centered and mean to my sister most of the time."

"But, as you said earlier, you and Tabby get along now, right?"

She nodded. "We're as close as any two siblings could be."

A strange look crossed Joe's face, and Lois wondered what he was thinking. Before she could voice the question, Joe said, "When I was eight years old, I went to Bible school. That's where I realized I had sinned and asked God to forgive me." He smiled. "Ever since then I've wanted to serve Him through some form of special ministry."

"Do you enjoy clowning?"

He chuckled. "Yep. I guess it's in my nature to make people laugh. I feel happier when I'm clowning around."

Lois was about to respond when Joe grabbed two straws from the plastic container sitting on their table and stuck one in each ear. "You think I could patent this?" he said in a teasing voice. "Hearing aids with no need for batteries." He shook his head from side to side, and the straws bounced up and down.

Lois stifled a giggle behind her hand. With his eyes crossed and two blue straws dangling from each ear, Joe looked hilarious. She was glad for those few minutes of finding out a little more about him. But she wondered if he ever stayed serious for long, and if so, would she find that side of him more appealing?

&

Joe tilted his head to one side and mentally replayed the questions she'd asked. She was not only beautiful but smart, and she'd laughed at his corny jokes and goofy antics. The only uncomfortable moment had come when she questioned him about his family.

He watched Lois drinking her lemonade. Her lips were pursed around the tip of the straw, and she drank in slow, delicate sips. *Wonder what it would feel like to kiss those rosy lips.* He gave his ear a sharp pull, hoping the gesture would get him thinking straight again. This was only their first date. He shouldn't be thinking about kissing Lois.

"You're staring at me."

He blinked then smiled. "Yeah, I guess I am."

"Do I have ketchup on my chin or something?"

"Nope. I was just thinking I'd like to get to know you better."

Lois nodded. "I'd like to know you better too."

"How about coming to one of my programs?" Joe asked. "I'll be part of a revival service at one of the largest churches in Puyallup next Friday night. We'll have performers from all over the Pacific Northwest." He smiled at her. "After the program, maybe we can go out for pie and coffee."

"Sounds like fun."

"So will you come?"

"I'd love to."

Joe smiled again, feeling as if he'd been handed a birthday present when it wasn't even his birthday.

seven

Lois sat spellbound as the gospel illusionist on stage at Puyallup Christian Church performed a disappearing dove trick. "After the flood, Noah sent out first a raven, then a dove, in search of dry land," he told everyone. He placed a live dove inside a silver pan, covered it with a lid, and opened it again. The bird was gone. A few minutes later, it reappeared inside the illusionist's coat.

Lois applauded with the rest of the audience.

After that, she watched two clowns perform using mime. Neither of them held her interest the way Joe did, though. They were more sophisticated in their approach, and throughout their routine they never uttered a word, as was the custom with mimes.

A group of puppeteers followed the clowns, and an artist did a beautiful chalk drawing of the resurrection of Christ. Lois thought of Tabby's friend, Donna, who also did chalk art. She knew Donna hadn't gone on tour with Tabby and Seth, since she had the day care to run, but she'd expected to see her here tonight. She thought Donna's drawings were every bit as good as the one being done now.

When she heard Slow-Joe the Clown being announced, Lois smiled. He was the main reason she'd come tonight.

&

Joe was comfortable in the costume he'd chosen—a cowboy clown suit, complete with ten-gallon hat, chaps, and bright-red leather boots. His red-and-white striped shirt offset his baggy white pants with red fringe sewn to the pockets and side seams. He wore his usual white face paint and red rubber nose, but he'd added a fake mustache to give him a rugged, cowboy look.

As Joe stepped onto the stage, he swung a rope over his head and hollered, "Yahoo! Ride 'em, cowboy!" Everyone cheered and clapped.

Joe threw the rope into the air, spun around as it fell to the ground, and shouted, "Now wait a minute! Where did that silly rope go? I had it in my hands a minute ago, and now it's disappeared."

When the laughter died down, Joe pivoted on his heels and tripped over the rope, which was lying a few inches in front of him. Next, he grabbed two folding chairs, draped the rope across the back of each one, then tied both ends in a knot. "Before I came out here, someone dared me to do this, so now I'm gonna walk the tightrope."

"Don't do it!" a child's voice shouted.

"Would you like to do it instead?" Joe called back.

"No, it's not safe!"

Joe eyed the rope. Then, slowly, deliberately, he lifted one foot, paused, and set his foot back down. "Anyone have an umbrella? I might need it for balance," he said to the audience.

"It's not safe!" the child yelled again.

Joe looked at the rope, tipped his head slightly, then bent to examine it more closely. "The rope looks strong, but the chairs might not hold my weight. Maybe I should do this the cautious way." With that, Joe quickly undid the rope, snapped it over his head, did a few fancy twirls, then flopped the rope onto the floor in a straight line. "Now it's safe!"

With exaggerated movements he stepped onto the rope, placing one boot in front of the other, and walked the tight-rope. When he came to the end, he turned to the audience and bowed. He heard several snickers, but nobody clapped. Frowning, he tugged gently on his mustache. "You didn't think that trick was impressive?" he asked the audience, turning his hands palm up. A few more snickers filtered through the room.

"I'll tell you what's impressive," Joe continued. "Doing what you know is right, even when others try to get you to do something that could be bad for you. Someone dared me to walk this tightrope while it was connected to two chairs. If I'd taken that dare, it would have been pretty stupid.

"God gave each of us the ability to discern what's right and wrong," Joe continued. "Even if you want to be liked and think taking a dare is cool, you need to use your brain and decide what's best for you in any situation." He pointed to the rope at his feet. "I don't have an umbrella for balance, the folding chairs aren't very sturdy, and I've never walked a tightrope in my life, so I decided to do the sensible thing." He turned and went back across the rope. "I walked a tightrope that was lying safely on the ground."

Everyone clapped, and Joe reached into his pocket to retrieve a balloon. "I'm going to create my favorite balloon critter now—Buzzy the Bee."

He inflated the balloon to make the insect's body, twisted one-third of it off for the head, then withdrew and blew up a second balloon. After he'd tied a knot, he formed a circle with the balloon. He twisted it in half to make two smaller circles, which would become the bee's wings. These were attached to the body with another twist. Using a black marking pen, Joe drew a face on the bee and rings around its middle.

"Whenever I see a bee, I'm reminded that God wants me to bee a good witness, bee kind to others, and bee faithful about going to church," he said, holding up the balloon. Joe stepped off the stage and handed the bee to the child who had warned him about the unsafe tightrope.

He ended his routine by spinning the rope over his head and telling the audience each of them had talents they could use to serve the Lord in some way.

&

Later that evening, at the restaurant where she and Joe had gone for dessert, Lois found herself once again enthralled with Slow-Joe the Clown's wit and goofy smile. "I could tell you were having fun during your performance tonight," she said.

"I always have fun when I'm on stage." Joe leaned across the table. "Speaking of fun, and changing the subject, I was at the mall the other day and stopped in to use the men's room."

Lois covered her ears with her hands. "Is this something I need to hear?"

Joe grinned. "When I was in the men's room, I noticed a sign on the wall, above a padded shelf. It read: 'Baby Changing Station.'" Joe shook his head slowly. "Can you imagine anyone wanting to leave their kid there, hoping it'll be changed when it comes out?" He chuckled and gave her a quick wink.

Lois groaned. "Don't you ever get tired of cracking jokes?"

"Nope." Joe reached for his cup of coffee. "So what do you do when you're not working?" he asked, changing the subject again.

She shrugged her shoulders. "I teach a first-grade Sunday school class, drive to Olympia to visit my folks a couple times a month, and read a lot."

"Nothing just for fun?"

"Reading a good book can be fun." Lois stared into her cup of tea for a moment, then glanced up and saw Joe dangling his spoon with two fingers, directly in front of her face.

"Very funny," she murmured.

Joe dropped the spoon and reached for her hand, and at once Lois felt her face flame. Was Joe flirting with her? The way he kidded around all the time she couldn't be sure if he was serious or teasing.

"The Puyallup Fair starts next weekend," Joe said. "Would you be interested in tagging along with me, maybe sometime Saturday afternoon?"

Lois nodded and smiled. They could find lots of fun things to do at the fair, and it would give her another opportunity to get to know Joe better.

"Great! I have to warn you, though—I get a little carried away when I ride the roller coaster, especially after I've inhaled a couple of cotton candies."

She gulped. The roller coaster? Surely Joe didn't expect her to ride that horrible contraption!

eight

As Lois and Joe headed to the Puyallup Fair in his blue pickup truck, a surge of excitement coursed through her.

"Here we are," Joe announced when they pulled into the parking lot near the fairgrounds.

Lois focused on her surroundings. She saw people everywhere, which was nothing unusual for a fair this size. Today it seemed worse than any other time she could remember, though. Maybe it was because of the unseasonably warm weather they'd been having in the Pacific Northwest. Sunshine brought people out by the droves, and something as entertaining as the fair had a lot of appeal.

Joe turned and grinned at Lois after he'd placed his parking stub on the dash. "Ready for an awesome day?"

She smiled in return. "Ready as I'll ever be."

Hand in hand, they made their way to the entrance gates. Joe bought two admission tickets, and they pushed through the revolving gate.

"Where would you like to start?" Joe asked as he grabbed a map of the fairgrounds from a nearby stand.

Lois shrugged. The crisp aroma of early fall mingled with cotton candy, corn dogs, and curly fries, teasing her senses. "I don't know—there's so much to see."

"And do," Joe added. "Why don't we start with the rides? That way we won't be tilting, whirling, and somersaulting on full stomachs or with our arms loaded with stuffed animals."

"Stuffed animals?"

He chucked her under the chin and wiggled his eyebrows, a habit she was coming to enjoy. "Yeah, I'm pretty good at knocking down pins at my favorite arcade game. Last time I came here, I went home with two giraffes, a sheep, and a huge pink bear."

Lois giggled as she tried to envision Joe carrying that many stuffed animals back to his truck. Of course, she reminded herself, he might have been with a date. Why else would he have tried to win so many prizes?

"You don't think I'm capable of winning anything?" Joe said, inclining his head and presenting Lois with a look that reminded her of a puppy begging for a treat.

"It's not that. I just can't imagine how you ever carried them all out of here."

"I admit I did have a little help. I gave one giraffe and the bear to some kids who'd spent all their money trying to win a prize and had come up empty-handed. The other giraffe and the sheep went home with me, and now they occupy a special place in one corner of my bedroom."

"So you have a circus theme in your room?"

"More like Noah's ark," he said, grabbing her hand again and pulling her through the crowd. "Which ride is your favorite?"

"Well—"

"Please don't tell me you like them all," he said in a teasing voice. "I don't think we have time or money enough to go on every one."

"Actually, the only rides I enjoy are the gondola, the Ferris wheel, and the merry-go-round."

Joe shook his finger at her and clicked his tongue. "All baby rides. If we're going to remember this day so we can tell our grandchildren about it, we need to do something really fun and exciting."

"Like what?" Lois asked, a knot forming in her throat.

"The roller coaster, of course!"

As they approached the midway, Lois grew more apprehensive. She hadn't ridden on the roller coaster since she was sixteen, and then she'd embarrassed herself in front of her friends. She could feel her fears mounting as she watched the cars climb the track, knowing they would zoom down and up again, and around the bend made her stomach lurch just thinking about it.

"You okay?" Joe asked with a note of concern. "You look a little green around the gills."

Lois swallowed hard, fighting down a wave of nausea. "I, uh, had a bad experience on the roller coaster one time."

"How long ago was that?"

"I was sixteen and had come here with a bunch of kids from my high school."

Joe nudged her in the ribs. "You're all grown up now, so riding the curvy monster should be easy as pie."

"Why don't you go on it alone, and I'll find a bench and watch from the ground below, where I'll be safe?" She nodded toward a mother and her two children who were walking by. "I'd much rather people watch, if that's okay."

"You can watch people from up there." Joe pointed to the climbing coaster, and Lois swallowed back another wave of nausea. "You'll be safe with me—I promise."

Before Lois could respond, Joe grabbed her around the waist and propelled her toward the ticket booth. "Two for the roller coaster," he announced to the woman behind the counter. Tickets in hand, he led Lois to the line where people stood waiting for the ride.

Lois wasn't sure what to do. She didn't want to make a scene in front of all these people, but if she rode on what Joe referred to as "the curvy monster," she was certain she would.

"Don't be nervous," Joe whispered in her ear. "Just hold my hand real tight, and when we're riding the wooden waves, scream like crazy. It wouldn't hurt to pray a little either," he added with a chuckle.

Standing in line, Lois's fears abated some. Being with Joe made her feel carefree, and his jovial spirit and playful attitude kept her laughing. But when they were ushered to the first seat of the coaster, her throat tightened again. What if she got sick as she had when she was a teenager? Or, worse yet, what if she threw up on Joe's white polo shirt? She decided to turn her head away from him, just in case.

"Smile—you're on Candid Camera," Joe said, reaching for her trembling hand.

She moaned. "I hope not. I'd be mortified if the whole world saw me right now."

Joe nuzzled her ear with his nose. "You've never looked more beautiful."

"Yeah, right."

"I'm serious," he asserted. "I love your silky yellow hair, and those bonny blue eyes of yours dazzle my heart."

Lois's heart began to pound, and it wasn't just because the roller coaster had started up the incline. Did Joe think she was beautiful, and had she dazzled his heart? With his clowning around so much, she couldn't always tell if he were serious or not. She didn't have long to ponder the question, for they'd reached the top and were about to cascade down the first part of the track.

"Yowzie! Zowzie!" Joe hollered as they began their descent. "This is way cool!"

Lois braced herself against the seat and held on tight. She screamed—and screamed—and screamed some more, until they reached the bottom and began to climb the next hill.

"That wasn't so bad, was it?" Joe asked.

Lois shook her head quickly, too afraid to speak. The truth was that it hadn't been as awful as she'd remembered. At least this time she'd managed to keep her breakfast down—so far.

"Here we go again," Joe roared in her ear. "Hang on tight and yell like crazy!"

Lois complied. It felt good to holler and howl as the up-and-down motion of the coaster caught her off guard and threw her stomach into a frenzy. It was actually fun, and she was having the time of her life.

At the end of the ride Lois felt exhilarated, instead of weak and shaky as she'd expected. "Let's go again!" she shouted.

Joe chuckled. "Maybe later. Right now I'm ready to ride the Ferris wheel."

Lois sighed. After their wild ride on the roller coaster, the Ferris wheel would seem like a piece of cake. It would be mellow and relaxing, though, and that was probably a good thing. It had been a long time since Lois had been this keyed up, and she was a bit concerned that she might make a mistake and blurt out to Joe how much she liked him. *I don't want to scare him away. He's too good to be true, and I need to go slowly.* If she and Joe were going to have a relationship, she knew it was better not to push or reveal her feelings too soon.

The day sped by like a whirlwind. They moved from one ride to the next and even stopped to eat barbecued ribs, coleslaw, and a huge order of curly fries, with lemonade and, later, soft chocolate ice cream cones. Joe won Lois a fuzzy, brown teddy bear and a huge spiral vase filled with gaudy pink feathered flowers. She loved it. The truth was that she would have been happy with a jar of old marbles if Joe had won them for her. Today had been like a fairy tale, and she wished it would never end. But it was getting late, and they both needed to be at church in the morning. She had a Sunday school class to teach, and Joe had told her he was scheduled to do a program at his home church in Olympia.

It was a little past ten when Joe walked Lois to her apartment door. She started to fidget. Would he kiss her good night? This was their third date, and so far he'd only held her hand, slipped his arm around her waist, and nuzzled her neck a few times. She didn't want him to see how nervous she was so she decided to ask him more questions about himself.

"You seem so naturally funny, Joe. I'm curious—did you get your humor from your dad or your mom?"

Joe stood there and stared at her while she waited for him to answer her question. She hoped he would tell her more about his family. Instead, he bent his head toward her and puckered his lips.

Lois held her breath then and closed her eyes. He was going to kiss her, and she was more than ready.

"Thanks for a great day." Joe gave her a quick peck on the cheek. "You were a good sport to ride that roller coaster with me." He squeezed her arm gently then turned to go. "See you, Lois."

Disappointment flooded Lois's soul as she watched him walk away. "So much for a perfect day," she muttered. Had she said or done something to turn him off? Maybe Joe didn't like her as much as she liked him. Would he call her again?

nine

Lois had given Joe her work phone number, hoping he might call during the day if he was busy doing programs at night. Four days had passed since their date to the fair, but still no word from him. The weekend would be here soon, and Lois was beginning to think she would have to spend it alone. Of course, she could make plans to visit her folks. They lived in Olympia, and so did Joe. Would that be a good enough excuse for her to drop by his house and say hello? Should she call first or stop by unannounced? What if that peck on the cheek and Joe's "See you, Lois" had been his way of letting her know he wouldn't be calling again? Even though he'd acted as if he enjoyed their day at the fair, he had made no promises to call.

She didn't want to scare him off. But if she didn't let him know she was interested in a relationship, he could slip through her fingers. She saw it as a no-win situation, and she felt frustrated.

As she prepared to leave the church after work on Friday afternoon, the pastor and his wife stopped her in the hallway. "Hi, Lois. How are things going?" Pastor Hanson asked.

"Good. Is there something I can do for you before I go?"

"No, but Norma just mentioned how you seemed a little down this week. We were wondering if you wanted to talk about anything before you head out for the weekend."

"Oh, well, I hate to bother you. You've both had a busy week."

"We're not in a hurry, Lois," the pastor's wife assured her.

"We don't have any plans for the evening."

Lois studied the floral pattern in the carpet. Should she tell them why she was feeling so uptight? She felt sure they would hold in confidence whatever she told them. Besides, she knew they'd counseled several couples recently, some married and some about to be. No doubt they had good insights on men and dating and how to know God's will for finding that special person. Maybe she should get their opinions about Joe.

Lois looked up and smiled. "Actually, you might be able to help."

"Let's go to the study then," Pastor Hanson suggested.

Once they were in the office, Lois took a seat across from the Hansons. "I've recently met a clown," she began.

The pastor chuckled. "You've just met a guy and already labeled him as a clown?"

Lois smiled. "No, he really is a clown." She leaned forward in the chair. "Joe Richey is a gospel clown, and I met him at a crusade at Westside Community Church a few weeks ago. He sort of fell into my lap."

The pastor's eyebrows shot up. "Oh?"

"You see—I told God that if He wanted me to find a man, He'd have to drop him into my lap." She paused then related the rest of the story, including the part about the little girl rolling into Joe and knocking him over.

The pastor and his wife laughed.

"That must have been quite a sight," Norma Hanson said.

"It was pretty embarrassing. Especially when Joe landed in my lap."

"I can imagine," she agreed kindly.

"After the program, Tabby and Seth invited me to join them for dessert at a nearby restaurant, and Joe showed up.

I was wondering if Tabby planned the whole thing, but she said no when I asked her a few days later."

Pastor Hanson leaned forward on his desk. "Changing the subject for a minute—and we'll get back to it—I was wondering if you've heard anything from Tabby and Seth since they went on tour."

"Only once. Tabby called to say their group was in Baker City, Oregon, and they were having successful revival services. She said they might stay on the road a few more weeks."

"That's good news. I hope the rest of their trip goes as well," Pastor Hanson said.

"So do I."

"Now back to your clown. What's troubling you about him?" he asked.

Lois drew in a breath and let it out quickly. "Joe and I have gone out a few times since we met, and even though I don't know him well yet, I really like him."

"Well, that's good, Lois. You know we were hoping you would get out more. I'm sure you're talking with the Lord about this."

She nodded. "Oh, yes. I've done nothing but pray. The trouble is that I haven't received any answers, and I'm not sure whether Joe returns my feelings."

"What makes you think that?" Mrs. Hanson asked.

"He dropped me off after our date last Saturday and, after a quick kiss on the cheek, said, 'See you, Lois.'" She swallowed against the lump lodged in her throat. "He hasn't called all week, and I'm worried he won't."

"Because he didn't say he'd call, or you're just not sure he will?"

"A little of both," she admitted. "Anyway, I'm planning to

drive to Olympia tomorrow, and since Joe lives in Olympia—"

"You thought you'd try to see him," the pastor said, finishing Lois's sentence.

She nodded.

"I'm not sure I believe it's always the man's place to pursue a relationship, though that's what worked best for Norma and me. And since I don't know Joe personally, I can't say how he would respond to your visiting him." He looked at her. "Did you plan to call first?"

"I don't have his phone number or address, so I'll need to get them from the Olympia phone book once I'm in town." Lois shrugged. "I'm not sure I should drop by without calling first." She looked down at her hands. "Besides, he may not want to see me anyway."

"Why do you think that, Lois?" Mrs. Hanson asked. "Didn't he enjoy your dates?"

"He seemed to, but then Joe always appears to be having a good time. He's a goofy guy who likes to laugh and make wisecracks and do silly things." Lois blinked against the burning at the back of her eyes. She didn't want to break down in front of the pastor and his wife. "Joe makes me laugh and feel carefree. It's something I've never felt with any other guy."

"Would you like our opinion, or do you feel better after talking about it?" the pastor asked.

"I'd like your opinion, if you wouldn't mind sharing it," Lois said.

"If it were me, I'd probably get Joe's phone number and call him. Tell him you're in town, and if he invites you to stop by, you'll know he wants to see you again."

"And I agree with Sam, Lois," Mrs. Hanson said. "I think that's a good idea."

Lois sighed with relief. That's what she had thought too, but it helped hearing it from them. Calling first would be much better than barging in unannounced. If Joe didn't want to see her, at least she would be spared the humiliation of looking him in the face when he told her so.

Lois stood up, a smile on her face. "Thanks for taking the time to listen."

Pastor Hanson smiled. "We'll be praying for you, Lois."

His wife gave her a hug. "Everything will work out fine. You can be sure of that."

&

Joe felt tired and out-of-sorts, although he never would have admitted it. On Monday he'd put on an hour-long program at a senior center, plus two kids' birthday parties the following day. This morning he had another party to do.

"Well, I'm glad people want me for my clowning and the balloon animals, especially for parties," he said aloud. "But I don't feel nearly as fulfilled as when I can present the gospel too. Oh, well, it does help pay the bills," he reminded himself.

He zipped up his rainbow-colored clown suit, recalling the squeals of delight from the younger children when he'd worn it to a party. He put on a fuzzy wig with different shades of blue and a cone-shaped hat streaked with lots of colors. Joe had contrived many of his costumes, most of them from rummaging through thrift stores. A professional seamstress at his church had made the other ones, including the one he wore now.

Joe remembered asking his mother to make his first costume. He knew she could sew and thought she might enjoy taking part in his ministry, but she'd refused and then scolded him for expecting her to work her "fingers to the bones" and get nothing in return.

"Did your love always have to be conditional, Mom?" Joe murmured as he studied his reflection in the mirror on the back of his closet door. "Couldn't you have supported me and offered your love freely?"

Joe stuck out his tongue at the clown he saw staring back at him. At least he could hide behind the makeup, which had taken him nearly an hour to apply. His nonsensical costume took only five minutes to don, but it made him appear to be someone else. From the minute he dipped his finger into the jar of grease paint and slapped some of the goop onto his face, Joe was in character. Even though he knew deep inside that he would always be little Joey Richey, who could never please his mother, everyone seemed to love him when he was a clown.

"Forget about Mom and how she made you feel," Joe said, as if he were speaking to someone else. "She's gone now, and it's best for you to put on a happy face." He smiled at the image in the mirror then turned to leave when he heard the phone ring.

"Joe Richey here," he said.

"Hi, Joe. It's Lois."

Joe felt his heart slam into his chest at the sound of Lois's voice. He'd wanted to call her all week, but somehow he hadn't found the time. "Hey, Lois. What's up?"

"I'm in Olympia. I came to see my folks and thought if you weren't busy maybe we could get together while I'm here."

Joe frowned. He'd like nothing better than to be with Lois. If he'd had his way, they would find something fun to do and spend the whole day together. But he couldn't. He had a birthday party to do, and afterward he was supposed to meet with someone at the hospital about doing a special program for some of the staff next week.

"I'm busy today, Lois," Joe said. Did she know how much it pained him to turn her down?

"Oh, I see. Well, I thought it was worth a try. Guess I'll let you go then. 'Bye, Joe."

"No, don't hang—" It was too late. The phone went dead. Lois hadn't given him a chance to explain. She probably thought he didn't want to see her.

"Oh, no! I can't call her back—I don't know where she was calling from." Joe snapped off his bedroom light. "I'll have to wait until next week when I can drive to Tacoma and try to straighten things out." He hurried out of the door, still wishing he could have explained.

❧

Lois left the phone booth and climbed back into her car. Feeling the weight of Joe's rejection, she let her head drop against the steering wheel. Each breath stung as she struggled to keep from dissolving into tears. It was exactly as she feared. Joe didn't want to see her anymore, and he was too polite to come right out and say so. If only he'd been more direct the other night when he'd taken her home from the Puyallup Fair, she wouldn't have called him at his home. He probably thought she was chasing after him.

She'd been foolish to let Joe steal her heart so soon. The happy clown's warm smile and carefree manner had captured her senses, but Lois knew she would have to be more careful from now on. She needed to guard her heart and her feelings.

ten

It was Monday morning, and Lois had been staring at her computer screen for the last five minutes, unable to type a single word. She needed to finish Pastor Hanson's sermon, since he'd given her his notes when she first arrived at work. She also had a stack of mail to go through, but Lois wasn't in the mood to do any of it. She was still feeling the pain of Joe's rejection. If only they could have met for a few minutes on Saturday, to talk and maybe share a meal. Would it have made any difference if they had? Tossing the question around in her mind brought no relief from Lois's frustrations. With sheer determination, she forced her thoughts off Joe and onto the work she needed to do.

By noon Lois had managed to catch up, and she decided to go out to lunch, hoping it would brighten her day. The deli was close to the church, and she could order her favorite veggie sandwich. She'd be glad when Tabby came back so she wouldn't have to eat alone.

❧

Joe hurried up the front steps of Bayview Christian Church. He hoped he wasn't too late. It was noon, and Lois might have already left for lunch. He drew in a breath as he opened the door, suddenly colliding with someone.

"Joe!"

"Lois!"

"What are you doing here?"

64

"I came to see you."

She took a step backward. "You did?"

He nodded. "I needed to explain about Saturday. You hung up before I had the chance to tell you why we couldn't get together." He looked at her. "Are you all right? I didn't mean to bump into you like that. I guess I was rushing too much."

"I'm okay. I'm on my way to lunch now," she said, turning away.

He touched her arm. "Mind if I join you?"

She shrugged. "I—I suppose we could talk at the deli down the street. That's where I was planning to eat."

Joe's stomach growled at the mention of lunch. He hadn't eaten a decent breakfast that morning because he'd been in such a hurry to get to Tacoma and see Lois. "That sounds good to me."

Lois led the way, and soon they were seated in a booth at the deli. Joe ordered a hamburger, fries, and a cola, while Lois asked for her favorite sandwich and a glass of iced tea.

They ate in silence for the first few minutes, and Joe used the time to study the young woman sitting across from him. A few pale freckles dappled her cute, upturned nose. Funny, he'd never noticed them before. *Maybe I should pay more attention to details.*

Joe knew he couldn't stall forever. It was time for him to explain about Saturday. If he didn't, they might spend the rest of their lunch without talking. He had a feeling Lois was pretty miffed at him. "I was on my way out to do a kid's birthday party when you called the other day. Later I had to see one of the men on the hospital board about doing a program at their staff meeting next week. That's why I didn't have time to get together with you when you were in Olympia." He winked and offered Lois what he hoped was his best smile. "Am I forgiven for not explaining then and for not calling after our last date? I was really bogged down all week."

Was that a look of relief he saw on Lois's face? She'd seemed so tense only a moment ago, but now she was smiling.

"Thanks for explaining, Joe. I thought maybe you didn't want to see me anymore or that you'd rather I not come to your house." Her gaze dropped to the table. "I figured you might be afraid for me to meet your family."

He reached across the table and took her hand. "I live alone. I have ever since my mother died from lung cancer a year ago."

"I'm sorry about your mother. I should have remembered you said both of your parents were gone."

"Would you like to go out with me this Saturday?" he asked, abruptly changing the subject.

"What did you have in mind?" Her forehead wrinkled. "I hope you weren't planning to take me for another roller coaster ride."

He shook his head. "Not in the real sense of the word. Besides, I think our relationship has already had a few ups and downs."

He saw her throat constrict as she swallowed. "Does that mean we have a relationship?"

"I hope so." He grinned and wagged his finger. "About our Saturday date—"

"Yes?"

"It's a surprise, so you'll have to wait and see where I'm taking you."

"At least tell me how I'm supposed to dress."

"Wear something casual. Maybe a pair of blue jeans and a sweatshirt." He nodded toward the window. "As you can see by the falling leaves, autumn is here, so there's a good chance the weather will be chilly and rainy."

"What time will you pick me up?"

"How does eleven o'clock in the morning sound?"

"I'll be ready."

&

An hour later, Lois was seated in front of her desk, feeling satisfied. Not only had she eaten a terrific lunch, but things were okay with her and Joe, and they were going out again. So much for her plan to guard her heart.

Lois tried to reign in her thoughts and concentrate on a list of names she needed to contact regarding church business, but an image of Joe's smiling face kept bobbing in front of her. She realized they had little in common, with his being a clown and her being Miss Serious. But he made her laugh, and she thought he could probably charm the birds right out of the trees.

Lois could feel the knots forming in her shoulders. She wondered if she'd be able to discard her fears and trust Joe not to hurt her. She hoped she could because she was beginning to care for him.

The telephone rang, halting Lois's thoughts. She needed to stay focused on her job. "Bayview Christian Church," she answered.

"Lois, is that you?"

"Tabby?"

"The one and only," her sister answered. "How are you doing?"

"Fine. How about you and Seth? Will you be coming back to Tacoma soon?"

"That's the reason I'm calling. We've decided to stay on tour awhile longer. I checked in with Donna earlier, and she says everything's fine at the day care."

"I've heard that too."

"Seth's a little worried about his ventriloquist shop, but he was caught up on all repairs before we left, so I think it will be okay if he's gone another few weeks."

"I'm sure it will be fine," Lois agreed.

"What's new with you?" Tabby asked, changing the subject. "Did that cute, funny clown ever call?"

"Yes, and we've gone on a couple of dates. In fact, he's taking me out again this Saturday."

"That's great. Where are you going?"

"Joe said it was a surprise." Lois drew in a breath then released it in a contented sigh. "I don't see how he could top our last date."

"Where'd you go?"

"To the Puyallup Fair, and Joe talked me into riding the roller coaster."

Tabby's sharp intake of breath indicated her reaction. "And you lived to tell about it?"

"It turned out to be a lot of fun," Lois admitted. "I think I've finally overcome my fear of the crazy ride."

"That's wonderful. I'm glad you and Joe are getting along so well. You two should be good for each other."

"What's that supposed to mean?"

"You tend to be a bit solemn sometimes, and Joe's playfulness will help you see the humorous side of life. Joe's a big kidder, so your serious side should give him some new perspectives."

Lois nodded, not even caring that Tabby couldn't see her reaction. Her sister was right. Lois definitely could use more joy in her life, but Joe more serious? Was that even possible?

eleven

As Joe prepared for his date with Lois, he began to have second thoughts. He enjoyed her company. More than he had any other woman he'd ever dated, in fact. He knew she was a Christian, and he was physically attracted to her, but something was holding him back. Was it the serious side of Lois that bothered him, or the personal questions she'd asked him? Joe never talked to anyone about his mother's emotional problems, his brother's leaving home, or even the details of his parents dying. It was too painful, and he'd found his own way of dealing with it, so why dredge up the past? Yet several times, when he and Lois had gone out, she'd brought up his family. So far, he'd managed to distract her or change the subject, but how long could he put her curiosity on hold?

Joe hopped into his truck and slammed the door. "Guess I'll have to keep her too busy laughing to ask any serious questions today."

❧

Lois grabbed her sweater and an umbrella from the stand. She'd looked out her living room window and saw Joe pull up to the curb in front of the apartment complex. It was fifteen minutes after he'd said he would be there, so she hurried out the door, glad her apartment was on the ground floor and within easy reach of the street.

"I would have come to the door to get you," Joe said when she opened his truck door and slid into the passenger's seat.

"I was ready and figured it would save time."

"Looks like you came prepared." He nodded toward her umbrella.

Lois glanced out the window at the cloudy sky. "Even though it's not raining at the moment, it could be later on."

"You're probably right," he agreed.

"So where are we heading?"

"Remember? It's a surprise."

Lois glanced at her blue jeans and peach-colored knit top. Joe had told her to wear something casual for their date, so she hoped she looked okay. He was dressed in a pair of jeans and a pale blue sweatshirt, which probably meant they weren't going anywhere fancy. Relieved, she leaned against the headrest and decided to enjoy the ride. She had a habit of worrying over little things, but being around Joe was helping her relax.

By the time they turned onto the freeway and headed north, Lois's curiosity was piqued. Were they going to Seattle? Whidbey Island? Vancouver? She was about to ask, but Joe posed a question just then.

"Heard anything from your sister and brother-in-law lately?"

She nodded. "Tabby called me the other day. She said their evangelistic tour has been quite successful, so they've decided to keep on going for a couple of more weeks."

Joe tapped the steering wheel with both thumbs. "That's great. Maybe I should have gone with them. It's always rewarding to put on a gospel program and see folks turn their lives over to the Lord."

"I've heard Tabby say that many times," Lois agreed. "Sometimes I feel jealous when she tells me how many people accept Christ after one of their performances."

"Why would you feel jealous?"

She sighed deeply. "My sister is using her talents for the Lord and helping people find a personal relationship with Him. That's part of what she and Seth do. I, on the other hand, have no talents to share."

"You're a secretary for the church, right?"

"Yes," she said, nodding, "but it doesn't seem like much."

"Not everyone has the ability to type, file, organize, and keep an office running smoothly. I'd say that's a talent in itself."

"You may be right, but it's not the same thing as what you and Tabby and Seth are involved in." Lois paused a moment. "Sometimes I think I should pursue some kind of Christian ministry that could be part of a gospel presentation."

Joe reached across the seat for her hand. "How about becoming a gospel clown? There's always room for one more."

She giggled. "Me?"

"Yes, you."

"I don't know the first thing about clowning."

"You don't have to. There are plenty of classes you can take. In fact, I'll be teaching one at a seminar in Bremerton next month." He winked at her. "It might be fun to have someone enrolled in my class who likes to ride roller coasters and eat cotton candy."

She swatted his arm playfully. "You're the one who likes to do those things, Silly. I was coerced into riding the roller coaster, and one bite of cotton candy was enough to last me all day."

"I stand corrected," he said with a chuckle. "Think about what I said, Lois. Even if you decide clowning isn't for you, I promise it'll be a fun class."

"I'll consider it. Thanks for telling me about it."

೩

Half an hour later, Joe exited the freeway and headed toward the Seattle Center. He was glad their conversation had been kept light and upbeat. Lois hadn't once mentioned his past. Of course, he'd kept her busy listening to his stories about the birthday parties he'd recently done, and then he'd told her several corny jokes.

"Ah-ha! So you're taking me to the Seattle Center!" Lois exclaimed.

"Yep. Sound like fun?" He glanced over to gauge her reaction.

She offered him a pleasant smile. "More carnival rides?"

"Nope—the Space Needle!"

Her mouth dropped open like a broken hinge. "You're kidding, right?"

He shook his head. "I thought we'd eat lunch in the restaurant up there. We can enjoy the magnificent view of Puget Sound."

Lois's face paled. "Uh, I really would rather eat at the food court, with my feet on solid ground."

Joe laughed. "Don't tell me you're afraid to go up in the Space Needle."

"Okay, I won't tell you that."

"Scared we might have an earthquake while we're in the elevator heading to the top?" he teased.

"I hadn't even thought about that prospect." Lois gripped the edge of the seat. "How about if I wait on the ground while you check out the beautiful sights?"

He shook his head. "No way! I planned to do something

special for this date, and I aim to see it through to the finish."

When Lois didn't reply, he glanced her way again. She was leaning against the headrest with her eyes closed. "Lois, are you asleep?"

Her eyes snapped open, and she shot him a pleading look. "I don't want to go to the Space Needle for lunch. I'm not up to it today."

Not up to it? What exactly was Lois saying? "Want to explain?" he asked.

"I'm afraid of heights, Joe. I have been ever since I was a little girl and my dad took me to the top of the Space Needle."

"But you're all grown up now," he argued. "And I won't let anything happen to you—I promise. Besides, you went on the roller coaster at the Puyallup Fair, and that's pretty high off the ground."

She shot him an exasperated look. "That wasn't half as high as the Space Needle, and it was moving at such rapid speeds. I didn't have time to think about how high I was."

"How about this—we'll go up and see the sights then come right back down and have lunch at the food court. Does that sound okay?"

"Lunch at the food court would be great, but I'm still not sure about going up in that needle."

"It'll be a breeze."

"Anything like riding the roller coaster?"

"You said you had fun."

"I did, after I got over my initial fear," she admitted.

"This won't be any different. Once you take in the beautiful scenery below, you'll be begging me to bring you back for another ride to the top of the world."

"Okay. I'm not thrilled about it, but I'll give it a try," Lois said with a deep sigh.

They pulled into a parking lot near the Seattle Center, and Joe found a spot before she could change her mind. He felt confident that once they were on the observation deck she would relax and enjoy her surroundings.

❧

Lois fidgeted and pulled nervously on the straps of her purse as they stood inside the enclosed area, waiting for the next elevator to take them to the top. "The top of the world." Wasn't that what Joe had called it? *I only hope I don't do something stupid up there. What if I get dizzy when I look down? What if I don't look down and still feel faint? What if—?*

Joe slipped his arm around Lois and tickled her ribs. "It's going to be okay. Trust me."

She squirmed, giggled, and tickled him back. The distraction was helping her relax. Each time Lois was with Joe, she liked him more. He could make her laugh, and he'd convinced her to ride the roller coaster. Now she was standing at the foot of the Space Needle. Was there no end to this man's persuasions?

The elevator door zipped open, and the attendant ushered them in. Lois felt herself being crowded to the back of the elevator, as the elevator filled with people. Joe's arm tightened around her waist, and she leaned into him and whispered, "I hope I don't live to regret this."

He chucked her under the chin. "You'll be fine."

"I sure hope so."

Without warning, Joe bent his head and kissed Lois's lips, snatching her breath away and causing her arms to go limp at her sides. Before she had time to regain her bearings, they were at the top, and Joe had pulled away.

"Here we are," he announced.

Lois gulped and took a tentative step forward. Mount Rainier and everything in the distance radiated beauty beyond compare, but the things directly below resembled ants, toy cars, and tiny buildings that looked like children's blocks. A wave of dizziness hit her, and she inhaled deeply, hoping to squelch the dizzy feeling before she toppled over.

"You doing okay?" Joe asked as he pulled Lois closer to his side.

"I–I feel kind of strange."

"It's the gorgeous view. It takes your breath away, doesn't it?"

She pressed her lips together and stood there like a statue.

"Come on! Let's go to the railing and see what we can see."

Before Lois could respond, Joe grabbed her hand and pulled her away from the wall where she'd been hovering. A few seconds later they were standing on the edge of the world. At least that's how it felt to Lois. Joe was right. The roller coaster at the fair had been child's play compared to this. Even though the rails were enclosed, Lois felt as if she might tumble over the edge to her death. No way could she stay up here long enough to eat lunch in the revolving restaurant!

"Can we go back down now?"

Joe didn't seem to hear what Lois was saying, as he whistled some silly tune and studied the panorama below.

Lois stood slightly behind him, leaning into his back, and praying she wouldn't pass out. She closed her eyes, hoping it would make her feel better, but the knowledge of where she stood was enough to make her head spin.

After what seemed like an eternity, Joe turned to face her. "Have you seen enough?"

Lois had seen more than she cared to see. She headed

toward the nearest elevator and was thankful they didn't have to wait as long as they had when they went up. She breathed a sigh of relief when the elevator door opened.

"That was awesome!" Joe announced as they stepped inside. "We were up so high I think I saw some of the passengers' faces looking out of the window in a jet that whizzed by."

Lois moaned. How could Joe make a joke at a time like this? Didn't he realize she'd nearly died of fright up there?

"Hey, you know what I think?"

She glared at him. "I can't imagine."

"Maybe we should go up in a plane for our next date."

"You have to be kidding!"

"I love being in the air. The only thing I don't like about plane travel is the waiting and, of course, having some airline personnel go through my belongings." Joe chuckled. "Airport security has been really tight lately. In fact, the last time I boarded a plane, they confiscated my most important possession."

"Really—what was that?" Lois asked, feeling a little better now that they were heading for solid ground again.

Joe's lips curved into a dopey little smile. "My sharp wit!"

twelve

The rest of the day in Seattle passed swiftly. Joe bought Lois a souvenir replica of the Space Needle, to remind her she'd actually gone up in it, and they ate lunch at the food court, sharing a Mexican dish large enough for two. After walking around the entire Seattle Center and enjoying the sights and sounds, Joe suggested they go to the waterfront.

Lois loved the salty smell of the bay and eagerly agreed. The next several hours were spent browsing the various gift shops, touring the aquarium, and finally having fish and chips at Ivar's Fish Bar. Now they were on their way home, and Lois dreaded having to tell Joe good-bye. She enjoyed being with him and wondered if she could love him. It amazed her sometimes that he could see the humor in almost any situation.

Leaning her head against the window, Lois closed her eyes and relived the memory of Joe mimicking the seals they'd seen at the aquarium. He'd done everything but stand on his head to get them to bark and slap their fins against the wooden deck when they begged for food.

"What's that little smile about?" Joe asked, breaking into Lois's thoughts.

She opened her eyes and glanced over at him. "I was thinking about how much fun I had today."

Joe grinned like a Cheshire cat. "You mean you're not mad at me for dragging you into the Space Needle?"

Her lower lip protruded. "Well, maybe a little. . . ."

"But I kept you well entertained the rest of the day, and you've decided to forgive me, right?"

She nodded and smiled.

"Maybe we can go to Snoqualmie Falls for our next date," he suggested. "We'd better do it soon, though, 'cause it's almost October, and the weather will be turning cold and damp soon."

Lois's heartbeat quickened. Joe wanted to see her again, and he was already talking about where they might go. "I haven't been up to the falls in ages. It's beautiful there, and we could take a picnic lunch."

His forehead wrinkled. "Since the weather is turning colder, and rain is a likely possibility, I'm not sure the picnic idea would fly, unless we eat in my truck."

She agreed. "A picnic lunch inside your truck sounds like a great idea."

"When would you like to go?" Joe asked.

"I'm pretty flexible. It's your hectic schedule we'll need to plan around. When will you have another free Saturday?"

He shrugged. "I'd better check my appointment book after I get home. I'll give you a call as soon as I know which day will work best."

"Sounds good to me," she said.

❧

Joe was glad they'd made it through the day without Lois's asking too many personal questions. Maybe she had given up on the idea of digging into his past and decided they could simply have a good time whenever they were together. That was all he wanted, wasn't it—just to enjoy Lois's company? No strings attached and no in-depth conversations about confidential things. It was too painful to talk about the past.

Joe had managed fine all these years by clowning around, and he wasn't about to let his guard down now.

"Would you like to come in for a cup of coffee before you head back on the road?" Lois asked as they stopped in front of her apartment complex.

He smiled. "Sure, that would be great." Joe hopped out of the truck and sprinted around to the other side to help Lois down.

As they strolled up the front sidewalk, Joe noticed a broken beer bottle lying in the grass. "Looks like folks choose to litter no matter where they live," he muttered.

"I know," Lois said. "My apartment manager does his best to keep the yard free of debris, but it's almost a full-time job."

Joe bent down to pick up the shattered glass. "I'll carry this in and drop it in your garbage can, if that's all right."

"Sure. It will be one less thing for poor Mr. Richards to face in the morning."

In Joe's hurry to retrieve what was left of the bottle, he didn't notice the jagged edge and cut his hand. "Ouch!" He cringed and dropped the piece of glass as a sharp pain shot through his hand then continued up his arm. "Guess I should be more careful when I'm playing with glass."

Lois frowned. "Here—let me take a look at that." She reached for Joe's hand, and a stream of dark blood oozed between his fingers and landed on her palm. "Oh, my! That looks like a nasty cut. I think you may need stitches."

Joe shrugged it off as though it were no more than a pin-prick. "Naw, it'll be fine once we get inside and I can wash my hand and slap on a bandage."

She gave him a dubious look, then handed over a clean handkerchief she'd taken from her purse. "Wrap this around the wound until we get indoors."

"What about the broken glass?"

"You'd better leave it for now. At the moment we have more pressing things to worry about."

Joe followed Lois to her apartment door. She unlocked the door and opened it for him to enter.

"I have antiseptic and bandages in the bathroom." Lois motioned to the kitchen table. "Have a seat and I'll get my first-aid kit."

"I can manage," Joe mumbled. "Just point the way to the bathroom."

"Are you sure you don't want my help? It's going to be difficult to work with only one hand."

He shook his head, although his hand was throbbing like crazy.

"The bathroom's the first door on the left," she said, nodding in that direction.

A few seconds later, Joe stepped into the bathroom, held his hand under the faucet, and turned on the cold water. A river of red poured from the wound. The room seemed to spin around him, and a wave of nausea rushed through his stomach. He leaned against the sink and moaned. "Guess I might need a couple of stitches after all."

"What was that?" Lois called from the other room.

"Could you come here a minute?"

She was at his side in a flash, concern etched on her face. "You look terrible, Joe. Maybe you should put your head between your legs, before you pass out."

"I can't stop the bleeding. I think you were right about my needing stitches." He smiled, but it took effort. "Guess we'll have to postpone our plans to go up to Snoqualmie Falls for awhile."

She looked at his hand and shuddered. "It's bleeding badly. I'd better get a towel." Lois opened a small cabinet and withdrew a bath towel. She wrapped it tightly around his hand and led him toward the door. "I'm driving you to the hospital, and you'd better not argue."

"I wouldn't dream of it," he mumbled. Funny, he'd never felt this woozy when he'd seen blood before. Maybe he was getting soft in the head.

Lois slipped one arm around Joe's waist, and they headed outside. "Mind if we take your truck?" she asked. "My car's in the parking garage, and I don't want to take the time to get it."

"Sure—that's fine. The keys are in my left pocket," he said as she helped him into the passenger's seat.

Lois pulled out the keys, hooked Joe's seat belt in place, closed the door, and ran around to the driver's side.

"St. Joseph's Hospital is only a few miles from here," she told him.

"That's good." Joe leaned his head back and tried to conjure up some pleasant thoughts so he wouldn't have to think about the throbbing in his hand or the blood already soaking through the towel.

When Lois parked the truck in front of the emergency room, Joe breathed a sigh of relief. At last he would get some help.

❧

After they checked in at the emergency room desk and filled out forms, Joe and Lois took seats and waited. Apparently, an accident involving three vehicles had occurred across town, and those people were receiving treatment now. The woman at the desk had told Joe he would be examined as soon as possible.

Lois recognized one of the nurses on duty as her neighbor

Bonnie McKenzie. She knew from the few conversations she'd had with Bonnie that she worked at St. Joseph's, was single, and dated often. Lois had seen more than a few men come to the apartment building to take out the vibrant redhead.

In a short time, Bonnie called Joe's name.

"I'll wait here, Joe," Lois told him. "You go on back."

"Oh, Lois—won't you come too?" Joe asked. "I'd really like it if you would."

Before she knew it, Lois was sitting beside the table on which Joe was lying, wishing she could be anywhere else but there. Hospitals made her nervous. They smelled funny, and most of the people who came to the ER were in pain— including Joe. She could see by the pinched expression on his face that he was hurting, although he kept telling jokes while the nurse administered a local anesthetic and cleaned the wound.

"I still can't get over the fact that Tacoma would name one of their hospitals after me," Joe said with a wink.

"What do you mean?" asked Bonnie.

"St. Joseph." Joe chuckled. "You know, if hospitals are places to get well, then tell me this—why do they serve such awful food?"

Before the nurse could respond, a tall man with gray hair entered the room and introduced himself as Dr. Bradshaw. Lois could see by the stern expression on his face that he was strictly business.

The doctor examined Joe's hand and gave the nurse some instructions. "Now lie back and relax, Mr. Richey. This won't hurt."

Joe's head fell back onto the small pillow. "That's because Nurse Bonnie has numbed my hand."

Dr. Bradshaw made no reply but quickly set to work.

Lois turned her head away and studied the wall. She had no desire to watch the doctor put stitches in Joe's hand, even if she was fairly sure he wouldn't feel any pain.

"This is like an operation, isn't it, Nurse Bonnie?" Joe asked.

"I suppose it could be categorized as such," she replied with a chuckle.

"From what I hear, the definition of a minor operation is one that someone else has, so I guess mine falls into the major operation category," Joe said with a loud guffaw.

Why is he doing this? Can't the man be serious about anything? Lois peeked at Joe, who was grinning from ear to ear. Nurse Bonnie was also smiling, but the doctor's face was a mask of austerity. *At least someone besides me sees the seriousness of all this.*

"We're nearly finished," the doctor said at last.

Lois breathed a sigh of relief, but Joe told another joke. "Does anyone here know what a specialist is?"

"Certainly," the nurse replied. "It's a doctor who devotes himself to some special branch of medicine."

"Not even close," Joe said. "A specialist is a doctor who has all his patients trained so they only get sick during his regular office hours."

Dr. Bradshaw groaned and shook his head, Bonnie chuckled, and Lois just sat there. *Maybe I'm too serious for my own good,* she thought, feeling her cheeks grow warm. *Bonnie obviously thinks Joe's funny, and maybe he's clowning around because it's the only way he knows how to deal with the pain. He could dislike hospitals as much as I do, but he sure does show it in a different way.*

The doctor cleared his throat. "Bandage this fellow's hand

then give him a tetanus shot, Miss McKenzie. When I looked at Mr. Richey's chart, I noticed he's overdue for one." He turned and strode out of the room.

Lois noticed that Joe's face had turned white. He pressed his lips into a tight line as the nurse stuck the needle in his arm. Afterward, he plastered another silly grin on his face. "Say, did you hear about the guy who was always getting sick with a cold or the flu?"

Bonnie shrugged her shoulders. "That could be just about anyone."

He nodded. "True, but this guy was shot so full of antibiotics that every time he sneezed he cured half a dozen people."

Bonnie laughed and gave Joe's good hand a little pat. "Be sure to keep that wound clean and watch for infection. If you see anything suspicious, get right back in here."

Joe hopped down from the table. "Sure thing, but I live in Olympia. So if I have any problems the hospital there will probably get my business." He glanced over at Lois and winked. It was the first time he'd looked her way since they'd come into the examining room.

"Ready to go?" Lois asked.

"Ready as I'll ever be. Sure am glad you're driving, though. My left hand feels like it's ten sizes too big with this huge roll of bandage Nurse Bonnie has slapped on me."

"It's for your own good, Mr. Richey," the nurse said as she led them out of the room. "Take care now, and, Lois, I'll probably see you around our apartment complex."

Lois waved to Bonnie and hurried out the door. She was anxious to get outside and breathe some fresh air.

A short time later Lois drove away from the hospital and headed for the freeway. "Hey—where are we going?" Joe asked. "Your place is that way." He pointed with his right hand.

"I'm taking you to Olympia."

His eyebrows shot up. "You're driving my truck—remember?"

"I know that."

"How will you get back to Tacoma? And where will you stay tonight?"

"My dad can pick me up at your house, as soon as I make sure you're okay, and then drive me back tomorrow. I'll stay at their house tonight."

"Why didn't I think of that?" Joe laughed.

Lois smiled. "You just had stitches—remember?"

thirteen

Lois woke up feeling groggy and disoriented. It took her a few minutes to realize she was in her old bedroom at her parents' home in Olympia. She yawned, sat up, and glanced at the clock on the table by her bed. It was almost eight o'clock. There was no way she and Dad could drive to Tacoma for her to shower, change, and still make it in time for Sunday school. She would have to call the superintendent and ask him to find a substitute for her class. If she left right away, she might make it for the morning worship service.

Maybe I should call Joe and see if he'd like me to go with him to his church this morning. Then Lois remembered she didn't have a change of clothes since she hadn't planned to stay all night at her parents' home. *The least I can do is give him a call and see how he's doing this morning.*

Lois reached for the telephone and dialed Joe's number.

"Joe Richey here." Joe's deep voice sounded sleepy, and Lois figured she had probably awakened him.

"Hi, it's Lois. I was wondering how your hand is this morning."

"It's still pretty sore, though I think I'll live." He laughed, but it sounded forced. "Thanks for coming to my rescue last night."

"You'd have done the same for me."

"You have that right."

There was a long pause. "Well, I should let you go. I need

to spend a few minutes with my parents then hurry back to Tacoma if I'm going to make it in time for church."

"I'd invite you to visit my church with me, but I think it might be best if I lie low today. The doctor said I should ice my hand if there's swelling and try to rest it for the next twenty-four hours."

"That makes sense to me," Lois said. "Is there anything I can do for you before I head home?"

"No, I think I can manage. Thanks for offering though."

"Guess I'll be seeing you then."

"Have a safe trip back to Tacoma."

"Thanks. Take care now."

"You too. Bye, Lois."

Lois hung up the phone and went down to the kitchen, where she found her parents sitting at the table, drinking coffee.

"There's more in the pot." Dad lifted his mug as she entered the room. Even with his paunchy stomach and thinning blond hair, she still thought her father was attractive.

She smiled and shook her head. "Thanks, Dad. I'd rather have tea."

"There's some in the cupboard above the refrigerator," her mother said. "What would you like me to fix for breakfast?"

"I'll just grab a piece of fruit," Lois replied. "Dad, can you drive me to Tacoma right away?"

His eyebrows lifted. "So soon? What's the rush?"

She took a seat at the table. "I've already missed Sunday school, and I'd like to at least get there in time for church."

Her mother sighed. "Church—church—church. Is that all my two daughters ever think about anymore?"

Lois held back a retort. Instead she smiled and said, "Have

you heard from Tabby recently?"

"She sent us a postcard from Moscow, Idaho, a few weeks ago," her mother answered. "Her note said she and Seth were extending their time on the road."

"I'm glad Tabby finally got over her shyness," her dad interjected, "but I don't see why she has to run around the countryside preaching hellfire and damnation."

Lois felt her face flame. Not too many years ago she'd have felt the same way about her sister. But now that she was a Christian, she understood why Tabby wanted to share the good news. "Tabby and Seth don't preach hellfire and damnation, Dad. They share God's love and how people can know Him personally through His Son, Jesus Christ."

Her dad shrugged and rubbed a hand across his chin. "Whatever."

Lois grabbed a banana from the fruit bowl and stood up. "Will you drive me back to Tacoma?"

He nodded curtly. "If that's what you want. You know me—always aim to please."

❧

It was harder to do things with one hand than Joe had expected. *Maybe I should've asked Lois to come by this morning and fix me a decent breakfast.* He shook his head as he struggled to butter a piece of toast. He hadn't realized until now how dependent he was on using both hands to do simple, basic things. "Guess it wouldn't have been fair to expect her to give up going to church and play nursemaid to me."

Joe dropped into a chair and stared blankly at the Sunday morning newspaper. He'd come to care for Lois. But did he have anything to offer a woman like her? She was sophisticated and beautiful and blessed with a sweet, Christian spirit.

She didn't seem prone to mood swings, which probably meant she was nothing like his mother. Still, Joe was holding back from any kind of commitment. What bothered him most was that he had no secure job, never knowing from week to week, month to month, where, when, or even *if* he would be called to do another program. What kind of future did he have to offer a wife?

"A wife?" Joe moaned. "Why am I even thinking about marriage?" After his mother died, he'd told himself he would never marry. Even though he'd been concerned about finding a woman whose emotions were stable, he was even more worried about his inability to support a family. Like Jesus' disciples, Joe lived from month to month on what others gave in payment for the services he rendered as a clown.

He glanced at his Bible, lying beside the newspaper. "I don't need to waste my time on these negative thoughts," he muttered. "I can look in my Bible for verses that remind me to have a merry heart."

⁂

Lois slipped into the pew, realizing she was ten minutes late, but glad she'd made it to church at all. Her dad hadn't been happy about driving her home before he'd read the Sunday newspaper. But at least they'd enjoyed a good visit in the car, though Lois was careful to keep the conversation light and away from religious things. It troubled her the way her parents were so opposed to church and faith in God and even talking about spiritual matters. She wanted them to see their need for Christ's forgiveness of their sins.

If Tabby and I keep praying and showing Mom and Dad we love them, maybe someday it will happen.

Lois opened her hymnbook and joined the congregation in

singing "Love Lifted Me." After a few lines, she felt her burdens become lighter as she thought about how much God loved her. Enough to send His Son to die in her place.

When the service was over, Lois spotted Tabby's friend, Donna, talking to the senior pastor and his wife. Lois waited patiently until they were finished, then she stepped up to Donna and gave her a little nudge. "How's everything with you?"

Donna shrugged. "Okay, but I'll sure be glad when Tabby's back. Things aren't the same without her, and the day care kids miss her something awful."

Lois was about to comment, but Donna cut her off. "Tabby really has a way with children. I think she'll make a good mother someday, don't you?"

Lois nodded. "I agree."

Donna motioned for Lois to move away from the crowd, and the two of them found a spot in one corner of the room. "So what's new in your life?"

"Well, I—"

"Hey, Lois, I'm glad to see you made it to church."

Lois turned and smiled at Dan Gleason, the Sunday school superintendent.

"I asked one of our older teens to take your class, and she said everything went fine," he told her.

"That's great. Thanks for taking care of things on such short notice," Lois responded.

"No problem." Dan grinned and reached up to scratch his head. "Say, I was wondering if you'd be interested in having Carla Sweeney help you every week. She'll graduate from high school in June and wants to find some kind of ministry within the church."

Lois smiled. She would love to have some help with her class. Sometimes she felt she had more kids than she could handle. An extra pair of hands would be helpful when it came to craft time as well. "Sure! Tell Carla I'd be happy to have her as my assistant."

Dan nodded, said good-bye, and walked off. Lois turned back to Donna, but she was gone.

Lois shrugged and headed for the nearest exit. It would be good to get home where she could relax for the rest of the day.

fourteen

Lois was sitting in front of her computer at work on Monday morning when she felt someone's hand touch her shoulder. She whirled around and was surprised to see her sister standing there.

"Tabby! When did you get back? Why didn't you call?"

Tabby held up one hand. "Whoa! One question at a time, please."

Lois stood and gave her sister a hug. "It's so good to see you."

"It's great to see you too. Seth and I got in late last night, which is why I didn't call. I decided to surprise you instead."

"You did that all right." Lois nodded toward the chair next to her desk. "Have a seat and tell me about your trip."

Tabby dropped into the chair and smiled. "It was awesome, Lois. Everywhere we went there were spiritual conversions. I feel so energized—I think I could hike up Mt. Rainier and not even feel winded."

Lois chuckled and gave her sister's arm a gentle squeeze. "Now that I'd like to see."

"Seriously, though, I wish you could have been there to see people asking Jesus into their hearts." Tabby's eyes misted.

"I wish that too," Lois murmured.

Tabby grinned. "What's new in your life? Are you still seeing Joe Richey?"

Lois nodded. "Up until last Saturday I was. I'm not sure about the future though."

Tabby's eyebrows furrowed. "Why not?"

"I'm worried that Joe and I might not be suited for one another. He probably needs someone more carefree and fun loving than I am. Maybe I should bow out, before one of us gets hurt."

"Bow out? You have to be kidding! I can see how much you care about Joe. It's written all over your face."

Lois hated to admit it, but Tabby was right. In spite of Joe's refusal to see the serious side of things, she was falling headlong into the tunnel of love.

"Did something happen between you and Joe to make you question your relationship?" Tabby asked.

"Sort of."

"Want to talk about it?'

"I–I guess so." Lois nodded toward her computer screen. "I really should get back to work right now. And you're probably expected in the day care center. Why don't we meet at our favorite spot for lunch, and I'll tell you about it then?"

Tabby stood up. "Sounds good to me." She smiled. "I'll meet you at Garrison's at noon."

Lois watched as Tabby left the room. Her sister walked with a bounce to her step and an assurance she'd never had before she started using her talents to serve the Lord. Talents. There was that word again. Lois couldn't help but envy others like Tabby and Seth who were both ventriloquists, Donna and her beautiful chalk-art drawings, and Joe with his gospel clown routines. What could Lois do that would have an impact on people's lives? Were being the church secretary and teaching a Sunday school class enough for her?

You could take the clowning class Joe is scheduled to teach next month, a little voice reminded her. *You won't know if you'd enjoy clowning until you give it a try.*

Lois grabbed her desk calendar and studied the month of October. She didn't have anything pencilled in, except a dental appointment, and the church harvest party. "I have the time," she murmured. "The question is, do I have the talent?"

⁂

Garrison's Deli was crowded, but Lois and Tabby found a small table in the corner. They both ordered veggie sandwiches and ate as they chatted.

"Tell me what the problem is with you and Joe," Tabby prompted her. "I thought you'd decided it didn't matter whether you and he were equally matched."

Lois shrugged. "I did think that for awhile, but the other night Joe cut his hand, and—"

"What happened? Was he hurt bad?"

"He was dropping me off at my apartment, and a bottle was lying in the front yard. When he picked it up, he cut his hand."

Tabby grimaced. "That's terrible. Did he need stitches?"

"Yes, and all during the process he kept cracking jokes." Lois wrinkled her forehead. "I could see by the look on his face that he was pretty stressed out; yet he kept making small talk and telling one joke after another." She sighed. "I guess he was trying to cover up his real feelings, but it made me wonder if he even knows how to be serious."

"Have you ever thought maybe Joe is so used to clowning he doesn't know when to quit? It could be that once you know him better, you'll see another side of the man."

"You think I should keep seeing him?"

"Of course. In the months since you and Michael Yehley broke up, I haven't seen you look so content." Tabby patted

Lois's hand. "Instead of hoping Joe will become more serious, why not try to be more lighthearted yourself?"

Lois contemplated her sister's last statement. "You could be right. Maybe I'll take one of Joe's clowning classes and find out how much humor I have inside of me."

❧

It had been a little over a week since Joe had cut his hand. The pain had subsided, and he was finally able to use it again. He'd had only one program in the last week, so that gave him time to allow the injury to heal—and the opportunity to think about his friendship with Lois.

Joe stared at his morning cup of coffee. Was their relationship going anywhere? He thought they'd had a great time at the Seattle Center last Saturday, but after he'd cut his hand and she'd taken him to the hospital, Lois seemed kind of distant. He hoped she wasn't prone to mood swings after all.

An uninvited image flashed onto the screen of Joe's mind, and a hard knot formed in his stomach. He could see himself and his little brother, Brian, sitting on the steps of their front porch. They were blowing bubbles and having a great time. Mom was seated in a wicker chair nearby, doing some kind of needlework. One minute she was laughing and sharing in the joy Joe felt as each bubble formed. But the next minute she was shouting at him. "Do you plan to sit there all day blowing bubbles, Joe, or are you going to weed those flower beds?"

Joe's throat constricted as the vision of his mother became clearer. She was wearing a pair of men's faded blue overalls, and her long, dark hair hung in a braid down her back. Her brown eyes flashed with anger as she jumped up from her seat, marched across the porch and grabbed hold of Joe's ear. "Do you hear me, Boy? Why are you wasting the day with those stupid bubbles?"

Tears stung the back of young Joe's eyes as he rose to his feet. "I—I didn't even know you wanted the flower beds weeded."

"Speak up! I can't understand when you mumble!"

"I didn't know you wanted me to do any weeding today," Joe said, much louder this time.

"Of course you knew. I told you that yesterday."

Joe handed his bottle of bubbles to Brian. "You might as well have some fun, even if I have to work all afternoon."

Brian's expression was one of pity, but he took the bubbles and looked away. Joe sauntered down the steps, as though nothing unusual had happened. In fact, by the time he reached the shed where the gardening tools were kept, Joe was whistling a tune.

The sharp ringing of the telephone jolted him back to the present. He was glad for the interruption. It always hurt when he thought about the past. It was difficult to deal with his pain over the way Mom used to be, but at least she'd committed her life to the Lord the night before she died. That was comforting, even though it hadn't erased the agony of the past.

The phone kept on ringing, and Joe finally grabbed the receiver. "Joe Richey here."

"Hi, Joe. It's Lois."

Joe's lips twitched, as he tried to gather his whirling thoughts into some kind of order. "What's up, Lois?"

"I called to see how your hand is doing."

"Much better, thanks," he said, flexing the fingers of the hand that had been cut.

"I'm glad to hear it." There was a long pause. "I also wanted to tell you, Joe, that I've made a decision."

A feeling of apprehension crept up Joe's spine. Was she going to say she didn't want to see him anymore? "What decision is that?"

"It's about that clowning class you'll be teaching in Bremerton next month."

Joe expelled the breath he'd been holding. "What about it?"

"I've decided to take you up on your offer. I want to learn how to be a clown."

fifteen

Lois sat in the front row of a classroom with about fifty other people. She held a pen and notebook in her hands and was ready for Slow-Joe the Clown to begin his presentation.

Joe swaggered into the room, dressed in a green-and-white checkered clown costume and wearing white face paint with a red nose. "Good mornin', folks! Glad you could be here today." He spotted Lois, waved, and gave her a quick wink.

She smiled at him but wished he hadn't singled her out.

"The first thing you should know about clowning is that clowns aren't just silly comedians who dress up in goofy costumes to entertain kids." Joe shook his head. "No, clowns are performing artists, and to be a successful clown you need to possess certain skills."

Lois stared down at her hands, now folded in her lap across the notebook. What skills did she have, other than being able to type eighty words a minute, answer the phone with a pleasant voice, and keep the church office running as smoothly as possible? She couldn't juggle balls, twist balloons into cute little animals, or think of anything funny to say. Did she have any business taking this class?

"The first recorded reference to clowning dates back to about 2270 B.C.," Joe stated. "A nine-year-old reportedly said, 'A jester came to rejoice and delight the heart!' Until the mid-1800s, most clowns wore very little makeup. Many clowns today do wear makeup, and each type of face paint can have some kind of meaning." Joe pointed to his cheek. "Take the white-faced look I'm wearing. Clowns who wear this type of makeup are usually the reserved, refined kind of clown." He offered the audience a lopsided grin. "Of course, there are exceptions to every rule."

Lois's hope began to soar. *Maybe I'm an exception. Maybe I can pretend to be sappy and happy.*

Joe moved over to the board and picked up a piece of chalk. He wrote in bold letters, "What Is a Clown Character?"

Lois smiled to herself. *You. You're a clown character, Joe Richey.*

"Each clown must somehow be different from all the other clowns," Joe said with a note of conviction. "Your unique personality is what will make you stand out from the rest. The makeup and clothes you choose to wear will enhance this creation. Your clown's appearance, way of moving, actions, and reactions are all influenced by your character's personality."

Joe seemed so confident and in his element talking about clowning. Lois picked up her notebook and pen again to take some serious notes.

"Next," Joe said, writing on the board, "ask yourself this question: What do I need to be a great clown? You could add some balloon animals to your routine. Or how about a bright orange vest? A few tricks? Juggling? A pet bird?" He shook his head. "While those are all good props and fun additions to your routines, the things you'll probably need more than anything else are improvisational skills, character development and, most important, a knowledge of the elements of humor."

Lois sighed and placed her notebook back in her lap.

Elements of humor. Sure hope I learn some of those today.

"Have you ever noticed how we often make assumptions about people based on what they are wearing?" Joe asked. "For instance, picture a man dressed in a pair of faded blue jeans with holes in the knees and a sweatshirt with a college logo on the front. He's wearing paint-stained tennis shoes and a wedding ring on his left hand, and he's holding a cup of coffee in one hand. What do we know about this person?"

"The guy's married and has a college degree, but he's too poor to buy new clothes," a young man in the audience called out.

"Could be," Joe said with a nod. "Anybody else have an idea?"

"The gentleman could be an educated, hard worker who likes to putter around the house," the older woman sitting beside Lois suggested.

Joe smiled. "You may be right. The point is, we can't always judge someone by the clothes he wears. His actions play a major role in defining who he is." Joe turned to the board and wrote, "Your character's appearance and personality must be consistent to seem real." He pivoted back to the audience. "If you dress in black, the audience will expect you to be an elegant or somber character, because clothing conveys a meaning. If you wear a baggy, torn costume, people will get the idea you're a hobo clown." He winked at the audience. "Since most clowns don't make a lot of money, this particular costume would be kind of appropriate."

Lois laughed along with everyone else. The concept of clowning was more complicated than she'd imagined it to be. If she was going to become a gospel clown, she'd have to come up with the kind of character she wanted to be. Next, she would need to find or make a suitable costume—one that would affirm the personality of her clown character. And that was only the beginning. She would still need to find a gimmick like balloon twisting or juggling—and be humorous.

Lois turned and glanced at the clock on the back wall. In fifteen minutes the class would be dismissed for a break. She wondered if she should head back to Tacoma or force herself to sit through the rest of Joe's class, hoping she might find some sense of direction.

"The more outrageous your personality, the more outlandish your costume should be," Joe said. "Contrary to popular belief, a good clown outfit is not a mixture of mismatched, odd-sized clothes. A costume you design, using your own choice of colors and prints, becomes your trademark."

Joe moved to the front of the room. "Here's an example of what I mean." He withdrew several balloons from his pocket, quickly blew up each one, and twisted them until he'd made something that resembled a hat. He then proceeded to add several curled balloons, sticking them straight up. He placed the hat on his head. The audience laughed, and Joe looked at the end of his nose so his eyes were crossed. "I'm so thankful I'm not bald anymore. Now I can change my name from Joe to Harry."

Joe Richey was not only a clown by profession, but he was also the funniest man Lois had ever known. Not that she knew him all that well, she reminded herself. In the short time they'd been dating, he'd told her very little about himself. She wondered why.

When the class was dismissed at the break, several people surrounded Joe, pelting him with questions. Lois knew this was her chance to escape. Joe wouldn't know she was gone until the next session began. She left the room, headed for the front door of the church then stopped. Did she want to leave? How would she know if she had the ability to become a clown if she didn't stay and learn more?

She turned and headed for the snack bar. She would grab a cup of tea and a cookie and march back into that classroom and soak up all the information she could.

The class was over at five o'clock, and Lois was tempted to linger. She wanted to spend a few minutes alone with Joe, but he was busy answering more questions and demonstrating some of his balloon techniques. She decided to head for home, knowing it would take almost an hour to get back to Tacoma. Tomorrow was Sunday, and she still had a little preparing to do for her Sunday school class craft. She would have to talk to Joe some other time.

❧

Joe thought Lois would wait after class, but when he finished talking to the last student he discovered she was gone. Had she been in such a hurry to get back to Tacoma that she couldn't even say good-bye?

He shrugged and grabbed up his notes. *Maybe it's my fault. I should have told her earlier that I wanted to take her to dinner.*

Joe was fairly certain Lois had enjoyed his class; he'd caught her laughing whenever he looked her way. He'd also seen her taking notes. Was she interested in pursuing a career in gospel clowning, or had she taken the class only out of curiosity?

Maybe she did it for a lark. Could be Lois has no more interest in clowning than she does me. Joe slapped the side of his hand with his palm. "Oh, man! You shouldn't have made any reference to clowns being poor. That's probably what turned her off."

Joe pulled himself to his full height and plastered a smile on his face. *Get a grip. It's not like Lois said she doesn't want to see you anymore. Besides, I'm supposed to be happy, not sad. Isn't that what clowns do best?*

sixteen

For the next two weeks, Lois studied her notes from Joe's clowning class, in hopes of doing a short skit for her Sunday school class. Joe had called her a few times, but he hadn't asked her out; he said he was swamped with gospel programs and kids' birthday parties.

Lois missed not seeing him, but she kept busy practicing her clowning routine and had even made a simple costume to wear. The outfit consisted of a pair of baggy overalls, a straw hat with a torn edge, a bright red blouse, and a pair of black rubber boots, all of which gave her a hillbilly look.

Finally, Sunday morning arrived, and Lois stood in the first-grade classroom, dressed in her costume, waiting for the children and her helper to arrive. She'd worn her hair in two ponytails with red ribbons tied at the ends, and had pencilled in a cluster of dark freckles on her cheeks and nose. In an attempt to make her mouth appear larger, she had taken bright red lipstick and filled in her lips then gone an inch outside with color. She also wore a red rubber clown nose.

Lois's main concern was the skit she'd prepared. Had she memorized it well enough? Could she ad lib if necessary? Would the kids think it was funny, yet still grasp the gospel message?

Feeling a trickle of sweat roll down her forehead, she reached into her back pocket and withdrew a man-sized handkerchief. She wiped the perspiration away and was stuffing the cloth into her pocket when the children started pouring into the room. "Look! Miss Lois is dressed like a clown!" one girl squealed.

"Yeah! A clown is here!" another child called out.

"Are you gonna make us a balloon animal?"

"Can you juggle any balls?"

"How about some tricks?"

The questions came faster than Lois could answer. She held up her hand to silence the group, looking around frantically for Carla Sweeney, the teenager who had promised to help. "If you'll all take a seat, I'll answer each of your questions one at a time."

The children clambered to the tables, and as soon as they were seated, their little hands shot up. Lois answered each child, letting them know she couldn't juggle, didn't know how to make balloon animals, and had no tricks up her sleeve. She did, however, have a skit to present. Relief flooded her when Carla slipped into the room, and before the children could fire more questions at her, Lois launched into her routine.

Using an artificial flower and a child's doctor kit, she did a pantomime, showing how the flower was sick and needed healing. She then explained out loud how the idea was compared to people who have things in their lives that make them sin-sick. "Jesus is the great physician," she said. "He will take away our sins if we ask Him to forgive us."

The children seemed to grasp the message, but they weren't spellbound, as the audience was when she'd seen Joe perform.

After class Lois washed her face, changed out of her costume, and slipped into a dress to wear to church. *Maybe I need to take another clowning class. I could learn how to juggle or maybe do some tricks. . .anything to leave a better impression.*

After church, Lois went with Tabby and Seth to dinner at a restaurant along the waterfront. As soon as they were seated, Seth informed Lois that this was the place he and Tabby had eaten after returning from their first date in Seattle.

Sitting at the table overlooking the beautiful bay, Lois couldn't help but feel a little jealous of her sister. She was married to her soul mate and glowed like a sunbeam. Lois knew she was still young and had plenty of time to find the right guy, but she didn't want to wait. She'd met a Christian man—one who made her laugh and feel accepted and who didn't seem to care about wealth, power, or prestige. She saw only one problem: Joe kidded around so much that she didn't think he'd ever take their relationship seriously.

"Lois, did you hear what I said?"

Tabby's pleasant voice halted Lois's disconcerting thoughts. She turned away from the window and offered her sister a half-hearted smile. "Sorry. I guess I was deep in thought."

"Tabby and I have an announcement to make," Seth declared.

Lois lifted her eyebrows. "I hope you're not leaving on another trip. I really missed you guys while you were gone."

Tabby shook her head. "I think we'll be sticking close to home for the next several months."

"Yeah—seven to be exact," Seth put in. He slipped his arm around Tabby and drew her close.

Lois narrowed her eyes. "I don't get it. Why will you be staying close to home for the next seven months?"

Before Tabby could reply, the light suddenly dawned. "Are you expecting a baby?"

Her sister nodded, and tears welled up in her eyes. "The

baby's due in the spring."

With mixed emotions, Lois reached across the table and grasped Tabby's hand. "Congratulations!" She glanced over at Seth. "I'm happy for both of you."

Lois was delighted to hear her sister's good news. It meant she would soon be an aunt, and Tabby deserved the opportunity to be a mother. But somewhere inside was her own desire to be married and have a family. She only hoped it would happen someday. "You'll both make good parents," she said sincerely.

"Sure hope so, 'cause we're really excited about this," Tabby said.

The waitress came to take their order, interrupting the conversation.

"I put on a little clowning skit for my Sunday school class this morning," Lois said, after the waitress left the table.

Tabby's eyebrows shot up. "Really? What prompted that?"

"I took one of Joe's clowning classes a few weeks ago."

"You never said a word about it," Tabby said, shaking her finger at her sister.

"I wanted to see if I could do it before saying anything."

"So how'd it go?" Seth asked.

Lois shrugged. "Okay, I guess. The kids seemed to get the message, but I think they were disappointed because I didn't do anything exciting, like balloon twisting, juggling, or some kind of trick."

"If you think clowning is something you want to pursue, maybe you should take another class or two," Tabby suggested.

"I hear there's going to be a workshop in Portland next weekend," Seth said. "A clown from Salem will be teaching the class. He has a bubble-blowing specialty he's added to his routines. Should be interesting."

Lois leaned forward, smiling. "I might look into that one. I think blowing bubbles would be a whole lot easier than creating balloon animals."

Tabby snickered. "As I recall, you always did enjoy waving your wand around the backyard and seeing how many bubbles you could make at one time."

Lois laughed. "And you liked to see how many you could pop!"

❧

Joe hung up the phone and sank to the couch. Still no answer at Lois's place. She should have been home from church by now.

Just then the phone rang, causing Joe to jump. He grabbed the receiver. "Joe Richey here."

"Hey, big brother! Long time no talk to."

Joe's mouth fell open. He hadn't heard from Brian in nearly a year. Not since he'd called asking to borrow money to pay his overdue rent.

"Joe. You still there, Buddy?"

Joe inhaled sharply and reached up to rub the back of his neck. He could almost see his brother's baby face, long scraggly blond hair and pale blue eyes. "Yeah, I'm here, Brian. What have you been up to?"

"Keepin' busy. And you?"

"Oh, about six feet two." Joe chuckled at his own wisecrack, but Brian's silence proved he wasn't impressed. "You still living in Boise?"

"Not anymore. I needed a new start."

Joe shook his head. *A new start, or are you leaving another string of bad debts?* He could only imagine how much his kid brother had probably messed up this time.

"I call Seattle my home these days, so we're practically neighbors."

"Seattle? How long have you been living there?"

"A couple of months." Brian cleared his throat. "I'm driving a taxi cab."

Joe wrinkled his brows. "You're a taxi driver? What happened to the sporting goods store you were managing in Boise?"

"I, uh, got tired of it."

Joe flexed his fingers. He thought his brother's voice sounded strained. No doubt Brian's previous employer had asked him to leave. It had happened before, and unless Brian learned to control his tongue it would no doubt happen again.

"If you've been in Seattle for awhile, why is this the first time I've heard from you? I was in that neck of the woods a couple of weeks ago and could have looked you up."

"Well, I've—"

"Been busy?"

"Yeah. Seattle's a jungle, you know."

"I can't argue with that." Joe's thoughts took him back to the date he'd had with Lois at the Seattle Center. He'd seen more cars on the road that day than he had for a long time, and people milled about the center like cattle in a pen. He didn't envy Brian's having to weave his way in and out of traffic all day, transporting irate customers to their destination.

"Listen, Joe. The reason I'm calling is, well, I was wanting to—"

"I don't have any extra money, Brian," Joe interrupted. "I can barely manage to pay my own bills these days."

"What bills?" Brian shouted. "Mom left you the house and

the money from her insurance policy, so I would think you'd be pretty well set."

Joe felt a trail of heat creep up the back of his neck. If Brian hadn't run off to do his own thing, leaving Joe to deal with their mother's emotional problems, maybe he would have inherited more from the will. As it was, Mom was crushed when her youngest son left home and seldom called or visited them.

Forcing his ragged breathing to return to normal, Joe plastered a smile on his face. He didn't know why, since his brother couldn't see him through the phone. Whenever Joe was riled, putting on a happy face seemed to help. It was the only way he knew how to handle stress. Besides, he wasn't about to let Brian push his buttons. One emotional son in the family was enough. Joe would keep his cool no matter how hard his brother tried to goad him. "Let's change the subject, shall we, Brian?"

"Did you ever stop to think I might have called for some other reason than to ask for money?" Brian's tone had a definite edge.

Joe snorted. "You never have before."

"You know what they say—there's a first time for everything."

Joe's patience was waning, and he knew if he didn't end this conversation soon, he might lose control. He couldn't let that happen. It would be a sign of weakness. He drew in a breath and let it out slowly. "Why did you call, Brian?"

"To wish you a happy birthday."

Joe leaned his head against the sofa cushion and chuckled. "My birthday's almost two weeks away, little brother. It's next Friday, to be exact."

"Next Friday, huh? Guess I forgot."

"It's no big deal." *Mom used to make a big deal out of her birthday,* Joe thought ruefully. *But she usually ignored Brian's and my birthdays.*

"Doin' anything special to celebrate?"

"Well, I'm hoping Lois and I might—"

"Lois? Who's she?"

"A friend." *A very special friend. But I'm not about to tell you that.*

"Where's the party going to be? Maybe I'll drive down to Olympia and join you."

"I'm not planning any big wing-ding to celebrate my twenty-fifth birthday. If I do anything at all, it'll just be a quiet dinner someplace nice."

"Okay. I get the picture. You don't want your loud-mouthed, hot-tempered little brother crashing your party. I can live with that. After all, it's nothing new for you to give me the brush off."

Joe opened his mouth to refute his brother's last statement, but he heard a click, and the phone went dead. "Now what I have done?" he moaned.

With a firm resolve not to dwell on the unpleasant encounter he'd had with Brian, Joe dialed Lois's number again. Her answering machine came on, and this time he left a message.

"Lois, this is Joe. I'm still pretty busy this week. I have two more birthday parties to do, not to mention a visit to a nursing home and a spot on a local kids' TV show. Things are looking better for the following week, though, and next Friday is my twenty-fifth birthday." He paused. "I, uh, was hoping you might be free to help me celebrate. Please give me a call when you get in—okay? Talk to you soon. 'Bye."

seventeen

It was close to six o'clock when Lois returned to her apartment Sunday evening. After dinner with Tabby and Seth, she had driven through Point Defiance Park, then stayed for a little while at Owen's Beach.

Dropping her purse on the coffee table, she noticed her answering machine was blinking. She clicked the button then smiled when she heard Joe's message asking her to help him celebrate his birthday. "I wonder what I can do to make it special," she murmured.

She reached for the phone and dialed Joe's number. She was relieved when he answered on the second ring. "Hi, Joe. It's Lois."

"Hey, it's good to hear your voice. Did you get my message?"

"Yes, I did. I just got in."

"What do you think about next Friday night?"

"So you need someone to help you celebrate your birthday?"

"Yeah, and I can't think of anyone I'd rather spend it with than you."

Lois grinned. Joe sounded sincere, and she was beginning to think he really did care for her.

He cleared his throat. "We'll get back to my birthday plans in a minute, but I've been meaning to ask you something, Lois."

"What's that?"

"I was wondering why you hightailed it out of my clowning class two weeks ago."

"I could see you were busy, and I didn't want to cut in on your time with the people who stayed to ask questions."

"I thought you might not have enjoyed the class," he said. "I was planning to ask you to dinner, but when I realized you'd left I figured the worst."

"The worst?"

"Yeah. I thought maybe you hated my class and didn't have the heart to say so."

Lois's heartbeat quickened. Joe had wanted to ask her out, and he thought she didn't like the class? She felt terrible about leaving him with the wrong impression. "I did enjoy your clowning presentation."

"Is it about the money then?"

"What? What money?"

"The fact that most gospel clowns aren't rich."

"Money's not an issue with me, Joe," Lois said, smiling. "It used to be, but not anymore. I realized it wasn't so important when I broke up with a man who had money but wasn't a Christian."

She heard Joe release his breath. "I'm glad we settled that." He groaned softly then followed it with a chuckle. "I've had enough unpleasantness for one day."

"What happened today that was unpleasant?"

"I had a phone call from my kid brother, Brian," he replied. "It seems he's left his job in Boise, Idaho, and lives in Seattle now."

Lois held her breath. Was Joe finally going to open up and talk about his family?

"He called under the guise of wishing me a happy birthday, but I think he really wanted money," Joe continued.

"Is Brian unemployed?"

"He said he's driving a cab, but from past experience. . ." Joe's voice trailed off, and he was silent for a moment. "Let's not talk about my renegade brother—okay? I'd much rather discuss our dinner plans for next Friday."

Lois smiled. "I'd love to help celebrate your birthday, Joe. How about letting me pick the place? I'll even drive to Olympia to get you."

"You're going to be my chauffeur?"

"Yes."

"Oh, boy! Does a white stretch limo come with the deal?"

She giggled. "I'm afraid you'll have to settle for my little, green clunker."

He moaned. "Well, if I must."

"I'll be by to pick you up at six o'clock sharp, so you'd better be ready and waiting."

"Yes, Ma'am."

Lois hung up the phone, feeling happier than she had all day. Joe wanted her to help celebrate his birthday, and now she could plan to do something special.

❧

On the drive to Portland Saturday morning, Lois was a ball of nerves. What if she took the second clowning class and still had no audience appeal? What if she lacked the courage to do a program in front of anyone besides her Sunday school kids? She knew she was probably expecting too much. After all, this would only be her second course in clowning, and Rome wasn't built in a day. She didn't have much time though. Joe's birthday was a week away, and she was determined to give him a surprise he'd never forget.

When Lois pulled into the parking lot of First Christian Church, she was amazed at all the cars. "There must be a lot of people interested in clowning," she murmured, turning off the engine.

Stepping inside the foyer of the large brick building, she realized why so many cars were parked outside. She saw that not only were classes in clowning being offered, but also ones in puppetry, ventriloquism, illusions, and chalk art. It reminded her of the story Tabby had told of her first encounter with ventriloquism and meeting Seth Beyers.

Lois stopped in front of the table marked "Clowning by Benny the Bubble Man" and registered for the class. A young woman dressed as a Raggedy Ann type of clown handed Lois a small notebook and a name tag.

A short time later, Lois was seated at the front of the class. *Joe would sure be surprised if he knew I was taking another clowning class. I'm glad he's not teaching at this seminar, or else he would have discovered my little secret by now.*

She forced her thoughts off Joe and onto Benny the Bubble Man, who with the help of his assistant, Raggedy Ruth, was demonstrating the art of making bubbles in different sizes and shapes. The pair expertly used a variety of wands and even a straw.

Lois thought it looked pretty simple until everyone in the class was given a jar of soapy liquid and instructed to make a bubble chain. She'd always prided herself on being adept at blowing bubbles, but her childhood tricks had involved making only one, two, or maybe three effervescent balls at one time. Making a string of six to eight bubbles was difficult, if not impossible. Even with Raggedy Ruth's help, Lois fumbled her way through the procedure. Something as tedious as this would take weeks, maybe months of practice, and she had only until next Friday.

"Maybe I should have taken one of the other clowning classes," she muttered.

"You're doing fine. Just keep practicing," Ruth assured her.

Lois was the last student to leave the classroom; she was determined to learn at least one bubble maneuver that might impress Joe and show him she could act as goofy as he did. If she could learn to be a clown, maybe Joe would start to show his serious side. It seemed like a fair trade to Lois.

eighteen

Lois leaned back in her office chair and yawned. How could she ever stay awake the rest of the day? For the last four nights she'd been up late, practicing her clown routine and blowing bubbles until her lips turned numb. She'd finally managed to make a chain of eight small bubbles and a bubble within a bubble, but she didn't think either trick was too exciting. Neither was her hillbilly clown costume.

Maybe I should forget the whole idea and take Joe to dinner as he's expecting. At least then I won't be as likely to embarrass myself.

Lois grabbed the stack of bulletins in front of her and started folding them. On the front cover was a picture of a nurse taking a child's temperature. Suddenly, an idea popped into her head. A new outfit—that's what she needed. A costume and some props. A small shop on the other side of town sold tricks, costumes, and other clowning aids. She would go there as soon as she got off work.

❧

Joe stared out his living room window. It was raining, which was nothing unusual for fall weather in the Pacific Northwest. He wasn't going to let it dampen his spirits, though. Today was his birthday, and he was going to dinner with Lois. *Sure hope she drives carefully on the freeway. It's bound to be slick with all this liquid sunshine. She should have let me drive to Tacoma and pick her up.* He glanced at the clock on the wall. *Five min-*

utes to six. She should be here any minute.

Joe sat on the couch to wait and turned his thoughts in another direction. He'd been presenting a program at a nearby nursing home the previous week when the son of one of the patients offered him a job. The man owned a hotel and needed several full-time entertainers. The position paid well and had some fringe benefits, but it involved secular clowning and would leave little time to minister as a gospel clown. He pulled out the man's business card and studied it for a minute. He'd told him he would think about it, but Joe knew he couldn't accept the position no matter how well it paid. He always seemed to need money, but his primary goal as a clown was to see people's lives changed through faith in Christ. If he spent most of his time entertaining, simply to amuse others, he'd lose precious opportunities to witness about God.

I'll call him in the morning and let him know I've decided not to take the job.

The doorbell rang then. He grinned. It must be Lois.

❧

Lois smiled when Joe opened the door. He looked so nice, dressed in a tan shirt, dark brown blazer, and matching slacks. He'd worn a tie too—a silly cartoon character standing on its head. "Happy birthday, Joe. You ready to go?" she said, reaching up and kissing him on the cheek.

Joe nodded enthusiastically. "Yes! I've been waiting all day for this." He drew her into his arms and kissed her upturned mouth.

"Are you having your dessert first?" she asked, tipping her head to one side.

He nodded and gave her a playful wink. "Absolutely! I may have more dessert after dinner, though."

Lois felt her cheeks grow warm. She hoped the rest of the evening went as well as these first few minutes.

"Where are we off to?" Joe asked as he followed Lois to her car. "Are we finally going to Snoqualmie Falls for that picnic?"

"Not tonight." Lois opened the door on the passenger's side and motioned for Joe to get in. "Don't ask me any more questions. My lips are sealed."

"You're going to chauffeur me, aren't you?"

"Yes, and you'd better get in before the rain turns us into a couple of drowned rats."

"It seems like ages since we last saw each other," Joe said as they started for the freeway. "I've missed you, Lois."

She glanced at him out of the corner of her eye. "Ditto."

"Anything new in your life since we last talked?"

"Nothing much. How's your busy schedule? Anything exciting happening in the life of Slow-Joe the Clown?"

"I was offered a job last week," he answered. "It pays really well, but I'm going to call the guy tomorrow and turn it down."

"Why?"

"It's a secular position that would take a lot of my time. I wouldn't be able to do nearly as many gospel presentations."

"I'm sure you've prayed about it," Lois said.

"I have." He reached for her hand. "Do you think I'm dumb for giving up the money?"

She shook her head. "Not at all."

Joe squeezed her fingers. "I'm glad you feel that way."

They drove in silence for awhile, listening to the Christian radio station Lois had turned on. When they left the freeway, Lois headed across town to the north end. Soon she pulled up in front of a quaint, three-story house with gray siding.

Joe gave her a strange look. "Where are we? This doesn't

look like a restaurant to me."

She smiled and turned off the engine. "It's not. This is where Tabby and Seth live."

"He has his ventriloquist shop in the basement, right?"

Lois nodded. "Have you ever been here?"

"No, but Seth told me about it. He said the place used to belong to his grandparents."

"Right again," she said as she unbuckled her seat belt.

"So what are we doing here? Are Seth and Tabby joining us for dinner?"

"Yes, they are." Lois turned in her seat to face Joe. "I hope you don't mind."

He shrugged and smiled. "Sure—whatever."

"Let's go inside and see if they're ready."

"Why don't I wait here and you get them?"

Lois knew her surprise wouldn't work if Joe didn't go inside the house. "Their place is really neat. I'd like you to see it," she insisted.

Joe was quiet.

"They have lots of antiques," Lois added, "and Seth has an old ventriloquist dummy he's dressed as a clown."

Joe undid his seat belt and opened the car door. "Okay, you win. Let's go inside."

They walked up to the Beyers' front porch, and Lois was about to turn the knob on the door. "Wait, Lois," Joe said, reaching for her hand. "There aren't any lights in the windows. Maybe they're not home."

"They're probably at the back of the house." Lois grasped the knob and opened the door. It was dark inside, and she grabbed Joe's hand then led him along the hallway, feeling her way as she went.

"Are you sure they're home?" Joe asked. "I don't hear a sound."

"Just hush and stay close to me."

They stepped into the living room, and in the next moment the lights snapped on. "Surprise!" a chorus of voices shouted. "Happy birthday, Joe!"

ॐ

At once Joe painted on a happy face and backed away from the exuberant people who had greeted him. This was a surprise party, and it didn't take a genius to realize Lois was behind the whole thing. Besides Seth and Tabby, he recognized several other people with whom he'd done gospel presentations. His biggest surprise was seeing his brother. Joe didn't know how it was possible, since none of his friends knew Brian. Other than Lois, he'd never mentioned him to his associates.

Joe leaned close to Lois and whispered, "How did my brother get here?"

She opened her mouth to reply, but Brian cut her off. "I'm here because she called around until she located the cab company I work for. I guess she thought you'd be happy to see me."

Joe swallowed hard and forced his smile to remain in place. "Of course I'm glad to see you. I'm just surprised." He gave Brian a quick hug, then turned to face Lois. "I thought we were going out to dinner."

Her face turned pink, and she squeezed his hand. "I wanted to do something different for your birthday."

Seth stepped forward and grasped Joe's shoulder. "You're lucky to have someone as special as my wife's sister looking out for you. Lois has worked hard planning this shindig in your honor."

Joe felt like a heel. He should be grateful Lois cared so much about him. He couldn't let her know how disappointed he was at not spending the evening alone with her. He reached over and hugged her. "Thanks for the surprise."

"There's more to come!" Lois said excitedly. "Besides the pizza, cake, and other goodies, I've planned a special program in your honor."

Joe raised his eyebrows. "A program? Now that does sound interesting."

❧

Lois breathed a sigh of relief when she realized Joe seemed okay with her change of plans. She hoped he would enjoy the festivities, especially since he always seemed to be the life of the party. She led him across the room and pointed to the recliner. "You sit here and visit with your friends while I go change into my party clothes."

He wrinkled his forehead. "I think you look fine in what you're wearing."

Lois glanced down at her beige slacks and rose-colored knit top. "I won't be long, and I hope you won't be disappointed." She leaned over and gave him a light kiss on the cheek then hurried out of the room. Tabby was behind her, and they both giggled as they started up the stairs leading to the bedrooms.

"I can't believe you're going through with this," Tabby said as she pulled Lois into her room.

Lois nodded soberly. "I hope I'm not making a mistake."

Tabby shook her head. "I don't think so. In fact, it might be just the thing that will bring Joe Richey to his knees."

"I don't get it."

"Knees. . .marriage. . .proposal. . . ."

Lois waved her hand. "Get real, Tabby. Joe and I have been

dating only since August. We barely know each other."

"But you're a couple of lovesick puppies," Tabby asserted. "I can see it all over your faces."

Lois shrugged. "Let's get my costume on and forget about love, shall we?"

A half hour later, the sisters emerged from the bedroom. Tabby went down the steps first, and Lois followed, wearing a nurse's uniform and carrying a satchel full of props.

She stood in the hallway, while Tabby stepped into the living room. "Ladies and gentlemen, it's my privilege to introduce our special guest tonight—the lovely nurse, Lois Johnson!"

Lois skipped into the room. "Is there a patient in the house? Somebody please provide me with a sick patient!"

On cue, Seth jumped up from his seat and grabbed hold of Joe's hand. "Here's your patient, Nurse Lois, and he's one sick fellow!"

Lois placed a chair in the middle of the room and asked Joe to sit down. Then she opened her satchel, drew out an over-sized pair of fake glasses, and put them on. Next she removed a rubber chicken and threw it into the air. "Oops! No dead birds around here!" she exclaimed. "It's my job to make people well."

She pulled a can of peanuts out of the bag and grinned at Joe. "I hear you've been feeling under the weather lately." Before he could respond, she tossed him the can. "Remove the lid, please."

Joe lifted the top, and a paper snake sailed into the air, almost hitting him in the nose. He stared at Lois for a second then burst into gales of laughter.

Lois dipped her hand into the satchel again and retrieved an oversized toothbrush. "Open real wide," she said, tipping Joe's head back. He opened his mouth, and she pretended to brush his teeth while she blew on the end of the toothbrush. A stream of bubbles drifted toward the ceiling. Joe laughed so hard his face turned cherry red. He thought she was funny, and apparently so did everyone else, for they were all laughing, clapping, and shouting for more.

"Now, sick patient, I'd like you to lie on the floor," Lois instructed. As Joe complied, she turned to face Tabby. "May I have the sheet, please?"

Tabby reached into a basket that was sitting on the floor and pulled out a white sheet. Lois threw the sheet over Joe, leaving only his head and feet exposed.

"I understand you're having some trouble with your left arm these days," Lois said, as she grabbed Joe's arm and raised it a few inches off the floor. Suddenly Joe's left leg came up, and everyone howled. She couldn't believe it; Joe was playing along with her routine.

Lois pushed on his leg, and up came the right arm. She shoved that down, and Joe's other arm shot up. They continued the game a few more minutes, until Lois announced, "I think this patient is well enough for some pizza. But before that I'd like to present him with a beautiful flower."

Lois drew a fake flower from her bag. Joe sat up, and she handed it to him. "Take a whiff and tell me what you smell."

Joe held the flower up to his nose and inhaled deeply. Lois squeezed the stem, and a stream of water shot out and hit Joe in the face. He yelped, then jumped up and began chasing Lois around the room. "I've always wondered what it would be like to catch a nurse!" he cried.

By the time Joe caught Lois, they were both laughing so hard tears were running down their cheeks. Lois had planned a few other things for her routine, but she knew she couldn't go on with the rest of the show. She didn't think she needed to anyway, since she had shown Joe what she'd learned about clowning and helped to make his birthday one to remember.

&

Joe couldn't believe how much he was enjoying the party. Lois was very funny when she decided to let her hair down.

"I didn't realize you'd learned so much about clowning during my short class," Joe said to Lois. They were all sitting around the table eating chocolate cake and strawberry ice cream.

She gave him a sheepish grin. "I took another class last Saturday in Portland."

"Ah-ha! I wondered where you were when I tried to call that afternoon." Joe needled her in the ribs. "Now the two of us can team up and do all sorts of routines at church functions."

"Speaking of church—have you found a church home in Seattle yet, Brian?" Seth asked, turning to Joe's brother.

Brian scrunched up his nose. "I'm religious enough. I don't need an hour of boring church every Sunday to make me a better person."

"Since when did you get religious?" Joe asked his brother.

"It's like this—when I drive my cab around the city, people pray a lot!"

"Yeah, I'm sure your passengers do pray," Joe said, forcing a smile. "As I recall, you always had a lead foot."

Brian frowned. "To be a cabby, you have to know how to move in and out of traffic."

"If you want my opinion—"

"I respect your opinion," Brian interrupted, "but I'd respect it even more if you kept it to yourself."

Joe opened his mouth to offer a comeback, but he felt Lois's hand touch his under the table. He wondered if she was trying to signal him to change the subject, so he squeezed her fingers in response. "This cake is delicious. Did you make it, Lois?"

She shook her head. "Tabby did the honors. I was too busy trying to come up with some kind of goofy clown skit."

"That nurse routine you did was pretty impressive," Seth interjected. "You and Joe work well together."

Joe draped his arm across Lois's shoulder and whispered in her ear, "We do, don't we?"

nineteen

Over the next few weeks Joe and Lois saw each other often. They visited Snoqualmie Falls and had a picnic in Joe's truck, drove up to Mount Rainier for a day of skiing, and got together at Lois's place to practice some joint clowning routines. On the night of Joe's birthday, he'd convinced Lois she had talent and suggested she use it to help him evangelize. Lois thought that after more practice she might be able to do some kind of routine with him.

She was still concerned about his inability to be serious, as well as his refusal to talk about his brother or other family members. She had noticed the way Joe and Brian related at the party and knew a problem existed between them. She kept hoping and praying he would open up to her as they drew closer to one another, but so far he'd remained the jokester. Her own clowning around didn't deter him either. If anything, Joe seemed to be even goofier. She worried that he might have something to hide, some family skeletons buried beneath his lighthearted exterior. She was concerned that those things, whatever they were, might put a wedge between them, either now or in the future.

Today was Thanksgiving, and Lois had invited Joe, Brian, Seth, and Tabby for dinner. Her sister had volunteered to bring the pies, but Lois insisted on doing the rest. She was eager for Joe to sample her cooking, and she hoped Brian's presence would help him relax and talk about his family.

By one o'clock, the turkey was almost cooked. Lois boiled the potatoes, then finished setting the table in her small dining room with her best china. The guests would be here any minute, and she was looking forward to the day ahead.

Seth and Tabby arrived first, bringing two pumpkin pies and one apple, along with a carton of whipping cream. "It looks like you've outdone yourself," Tabby said as she studied the table.

Lois smiled and took one of the pies from her sister. "It's my first attempt at holiday entertaining, and I wanted everything to be perfect."

Seth whistled. "If the smell of that bird is any indication of what dinner's going to taste like, then I'd say everything will be more than perfect."

Lois winked at her brother-in-law and motioned toward the couch. "Have a seat, and when Joe and his brother arrive you can keep them entertained." She nodded at Tabby. "The two of us have some work to do in the other room."

Tabby set her pies on the countertop and grabbed one of Lois's aprons from a drawer. "What would you like me to do first?"

"How about mashing the potatoes while I make some gravy?"

"I think I can manage that."

Lois noticed that Tabby's stomach was protruding slightly, and a pang of jealousy stabbed her heart. What if she never married or had any children? Could she learn to be content with being an aunt? *I don't need to think about this now,* she chided herself. *There's too much to do.* She focused her thoughts on stirring the gravy.

By the time Lois and Tabby were ready to serve dinner, Joe

and Brian arrived. They hadn't come together, but Lois figured that was because Joe had been driving from Olympia and his brother from Seattle, which was in the opposite direction.

Joe greeted Lois with a kiss on the cheek, and soon everyone was seated at the table. Lois asked Seth to say the blessing then excused herself to bring in the turkey. Moments later she placed the platter in front of Joe amidst everyone's oohs and ahhs and asked if he would carve the bird.

"You picked the right guy for the job," he said with a grin. "When Brian and I were growing up, carving the bird was always my responsibility."

"Did your dad teach you how?" Tabby inquired.

"He was killed in an accident involving the tour bus Dad drove. Joe and I were both kids," Brian answered before his brother could open his mouth. "I hardly remember our father."

"My folks died when I was pretty young too," Seth said. "Grandma and Grandpa Beyers raised me after Mom and Dad were killed. Then later, when they decided to move to a retirement center, they gave me their home."

"After Dad's death, our mother raised us." Brian frowned. "At least that's what she thought she was doing."

Lois's interest was piqued. What did Brian mean by saying his mother *thought* she was raising them? She turned to him. "It must have been hard for your mother to raise two boys without a father. I'm sure she did the best she could."

Brian snorted and reached for a biscuit from the basket in the center of the table. "If Mom had done the best she could, she would have admitted she was sick and taken the medicine the doctor prescribed. Now she's dead, and we're left with only each other and a lot of bad memories."

Lois glanced at Joe, sitting on the other side of her, and

hoped he would add something to Brian's comment.

Joe was silent. With a silly grin plastered on his face, he reached for the tray of fresh vegetables, grabbed a cherry tomato, poked a hole in one end, then stuck the whole thing on the tip of his nose. "How's this for a new clown face?" he asked with a chuckle. He reached into the tray again and withdrew two cucumber slices. He cut a hole in each one then placed them over his ears. Next he grabbed a carrot and stuck that in his mouth. "What'd ya think ub this?" he mumbled.

Everyone but Brian laughed at Joe's silly antics. "If you don't want to discuss our mother's problems, that's fine—but let's not make these folks think you're ready for the loony bin as well," Brian said.

The carrot dropped to his plate as Joe opened his mouth. "I don't think we should be having this discussion right now. Today's Thanksgiving, and we ought to be concentrating on having a good time and being thankful for all we have, instead of talking about someone who made her peace with God and isn't here to defend herself."

Joe's face was as red as the tomato still dangling from his nose, and Lois wondered what she could do to help ease the tension. She offered up a quick prayer then reached over and took his hand. "Maybe after dinner you can do one of your juggling routines. In the meantime, how about slicing that turkey before we all starve?"

Joe snatched both cucumbers off his ears and the tomato from his nose and placed them on the edge of his plate. Without another word, he grabbed the knife and stuck it into the bird.

❧

Joe's insides were churning like a blender running on full

speed. How dare his brother air their family's dirty laundry in front of Lois and her relatives! If he hadn't been trying so hard to keep his emotions in check, he might have shouted at Brian to shut up and eat, rather than make himself look foolish by putting on a vegetable clown face. Lois probably thought he was the one with a mental problem. Keeping control of his emotions was important to Joe. If he acted on his feelings, he might flip out, the way Mom had on more than one occasion.

Joe found himself beginning to care more and more for Lois, and he didn't want to turn her off by losing his cool—or by revealing too much about his family. Making a joke out of things was the only way he knew how to cope with the unpleasant things in life. It was better than turning to drugs or alcohol, as Brian had when he was a teenager. Joe hoped his brother had given up those bad habits, but after today it was obvious he still hadn't learned to control his tongue.

Many times when they were growing up Brian had blurted out something to someone about their mother and her mood swings. Joe had tried then to talk to him about keeping their family affairs quiet, but his little brother seemed to take pleasure in letting everyone know their mother had a serious problem. When Brian finally graduated from high school and left home, Joe hated to admit he was relieved. At least his brother could no longer talk about their personal lives. Joe felt a sense of duty to Mom and had continued to live with her until she died. In all that time, he'd never told anyone about her problem with extreme mood swings or discussed the way it had made him feel.

"When's your next performance, Joe?"

Seth's question drew Joe out of his reflections, and he

smiled and passed him the plate of turkey. "I'm scheduled to do one tomorrow at the Tacoma Mall. It's part of the pre-Christmas festivities, and I'll be making some balloon animals to give out to the children who visit Santa."

"Sounds pretty corny if you ask me," Brian muttered. "If I had a choice, I'd choose driving in and out of traffic all day rather than spend five minutes with a bunch of runny-nosed, rowdy kids."

All eyes were focused on Brian. Joe knew Tabby and Seth were expecting a baby in the spring and that Lois loved kids. He could only imagine what Lois and her family must think of his self-centered brother.

"Kids and laughter are what makes the world go around," Joe said. "I love working with the little tykes because they spread happiness, peanut butter, and chicken pox."

Brian frowned. "Humph! And that coming from someone who's a big kid himself! You were always Mom's funny little boy, full of jokes and wisecracks, and never wanting to rock the boat or make any waves."

Joe inhaled sharply. He thought about telling Brian he'd made up a new beatitude: "Blessed are they who have nothing to say and can't be persuaded to say it."

Just then Seth spoke up.

"The turkey is great, Lois. You really outdid yourself."

"Yes, everything tastes wonderful," Tabby agreed.

Lois smiled, and her face turned pink. "Thanks."

Joe patted his stomach. "They're right; the meal was terrific. In fact, tomorrow I'll probably have to go on a diet." He winked at Lois. "Whenever I have to start applying my clown makeup with a paint roller, I know it's time to lose weight."

Everyone, except Brian, laughed at Joe's joke. He was eating mashed potatoes at lightning speed. *That's okay,* Joe mused. Brian never did appreciate a good pun. *Maybe I should try another one and see if that gets any response.*

"You look kind of stressed out, Brian. Must be ready for those tasty desserts Tabby brought, huh?"

His brother's forehead wrinkled, but he remained silent.

Joe chuckled. "Stressed spelled backwards is desserts."

Again, everyone but Brian laughed. Instead he narrowed his eyes at Joe. "You're really sick, you know that? I don't see how anyone as beautiful and intelligent as Lois could put up with you clowning around all the time."

Brian's words pierced Joe. He wondered if Lois felt the same way about his silliness. If she did, she'd never said anything. In fact, she was learning to be a clown herself, so that must mean she liked his goofy ways and wanted to be more like him—didn't it?

twenty

As Lois put away the last of the clean dishes from their Thanksgiving meal, her mind wandered. Joe's brother had revealed some important things about their past, including that their mother had suffered with a mental illness. Could that be why Joe was reluctant to talk about his family? Maybe it was also why Joe showed only his silly side. Lois had a hunch Joe had a lot of pain bottled up inside and for some reason was afraid to let it out. She wondered what it would take to break down the walls he'd built up. She wished he'd stayed around after the others left, but he was the first person to say he needed to leave.

Lois had no idea why Joe needed to go home, since today was a holiday and he had no clowning engagements scheduled. She'd tried to talk to him for a few minutes in front of her apartment building, but he'd hurried away, mumbling something about the ocean calling to him.

She sank into a chair at the kitchen table and closed her eyes. She could still picture Joe sitting at her dining room table during dinner, leaning slightly forward. His pinched face and forced smile betrayed the tension he must have felt when Brian began talking about their mother's condition.

"Dear Lord," Lois prayed, "I think Joe is deeply troubled and needs Your help. Please show me if there's something I can do."

❧

Joe had intended to go home after he left Lois's, but he

135

couldn't face his empty house tonight. Not when he had Mom on his mind. He drove past the Olympia exit and headed toward the coast. Maybe he would feel better after some time at the beach. A blast of salt sea air and the cold sand sifting into his sneakers would get him thinking straight again. So what if he only had the clothes on his back and no toothbrush? If he stayed more than a day he could buy what he needed.

"Lord, I've blown it with Lois," Joe prayed. "I could see by the look on her face during dinner that she's fed up with me. Did hearing about Mom's problems turn her off, or was she irritated because I wouldn't hang around and talk?"

Joe's stomach ached from holding back his feelings. He wanted to pull his truck to the side of the road, drop his head onto the steering wheel, and let the tears that had built up through the years spill over like water released from a dam. He couldn't, though. He had to keep driving until the Pacific Ocean came into view. He needed to drown out the past. Joe didn't care that by leaving town he'd have to cancel the performance he was scheduled to give at the Tacoma Mall the next afternoon. So what if they never asked him to do another clowning routine? Right now he didn't care if he ever worked again.

&

Lois hadn't heard anything from Joe since Thanksgiving, and now it was Friday of the following week. She'd been tempted to call several times but decided she should give him more time to make the first move.

She turned off her computer and was about to call it a day when the pastor's wife entered her office.

"How are things going, Lois?" she asked. "Do you and your

clown friend have big plans for the weekend?"

"It's going okay here at work." Lois swallowed against the knot in her throat. "I haven't heard from Joe all week, and frankly I wonder if he will ever call again."

Norma Hanson slipped into the chair beside Lois's desk. "Would you like to talk about it?"

Lois hesitated then took a deep breath. "I found out Thanksgiving that his mother had severe mood swings, and he acted strange after his brother blurted out the information." She sighed. "I think Joe's past might have something to do with the way he makes light of everything."

The pastor's wife handed Lois a tissue from the box on her desk. "Does Joe's humor bother you?"

Lois smiled through her tears. "Actually, I think he's been good for me, and his joking has helped me learn to relax and have a good time." She paused. "I just wish he could show his serious side too. If he even has one, that is."

The older woman nodded. "I'm sure he does. Maybe he needs more time. Perhaps as your friendship grows, he'll open up to you more."

"I hope so, Mrs. Hanson." Lois reached for her purse. "Well, I mustn't take up any more of your time."

"I'm glad to listen anytime and even offer an opinion if you ask," she said, smiling. "Before you go, though, let's have a word of prayer."

28

A whole week at the beach, and Joe still felt as if his world were tilting precariously. He couldn't afford to spend any more nights in a hotel, and it wasn't warm enough to pitch a tent on the sand. Besides, he was expected to perform at his home church on Sunday morning. It was bad enough he'd missed the mall program right after Thanksgiving. He certainly wouldn't feel right about leaving Pastor Cummings in the lurch. Especially when his clowning skit was supposed to be the children's sermon for the day and coincide with the pastor's message.

With his mood matching that of the overcast sky, Joe climbed into his pickup on Saturday morning and headed home.

On Sunday morning, he was still struggling with feelings he kept pushing down. He was determined to put on a happy face and act as if nothing were wrong.

Checking to see that his chaps were in place and donning his floppy red cowboy hat, he entered the sanctuary through a side door near the pulpit.

"Howdy, Pardners!" Joe shouted as he sprinted onto the platform, twirling a rope over his head. "Anyone know what the rope said to the knot?"

When no one responded, Joe said, "You're naughty!"

Several children in the front row giggled, and Joe winked at them. "Today we'll be talking about witnessing and inviting our friends to church," he announced. "I'll need a helper though. Any volunteers?"

A few hands shot up, and Joe pointed to a young boy. "What's your name?"

"Billy," the boy told him.

"Well, come on up, Billy, and stand right over there." Joe pointed to the spot where he wanted Billy to stand then took several steps backward. "Now let's think of some ways we can witness to our friends about Jesus." In one quick motion, Joe twirled his rope, flung it over the boy's head, and cinched it around his waist. "There! I've roped you real good, and now you've gotta listen to the pastor's message."

Billy looked at Joe as if he'd taken leave of his senses. "Guess ropin' your friends isn't the best way to invite them to church." He undid the rope. "Hmm. . .what else could I do to get someone to come to church?"

Joe tipped his head to one side, pressed his lips together, then snapped his fingers. "I know! I'll handcuff this young man and force him to come to church." Joe reached into his back pocket and pulled out a pair of plastic handcuffs. He dangled them above Billy's head, and several children laughed. "You don't think that's a good idea?"

"That wouldn't be nice!" a little girl shouted.

Joe nodded. "You're right. It wouldn't be." He tapped the toe of his cowboy boot against the floor. "Let's see now." Joe bent down so he was on the same level with the boy. "If you're not willing to go to Sunday school with me, I won't be your friend anymore."

Billy raised his eyebrows. Joe chuckled then ruffled the child's hair. "Guess that's not the way to witness either."

Joe began to pace the length of the platform. "What's the best way to witness? What's the best way to witness?" He stopped suddenly, nearly running into the boy. "Hey! You still here?"

Billy nodded. "Do you want me to sit down?"

Joe shook his head. "No way! We still haven't shown these kids the best way to witness."

Billy tapped Joe on the arm, and Joe bent down so the boy could whisper something in his ear. When he lifted his head again, Joe was smiling. He turned to face the audience. "This young man thinks I should offer him something so he'll agree to come to Sunday school with me." He winked. "And I think

I have the perfect gift."

Joe reached into another pocket of his baggy jeans and grabbed a couple of pencil balloons. The first one he inflated flew across the room, and everyone howled. When he blew up the next one, he twisted it quickly into an animal. "Here you go, Son—your very own pony." He handed Billy the balloon creation then told him he could return to his seat.

Next Joe pulled a small New Testament from his shirt pocket. He opened it and turned a few pages. "In Mark, chapter 16, verse 15, Jesus commanded His disciples to go into the world and preach the good news to all creation." He held up the book. "That means we should do the same. We need to tell others about Jesus, and one of the ways we can do that is by inviting our friends and relatives to Sunday school and church where they can hear Bible stories about Him."

Joe moved to the end of the platform and held up the rope and handcuffs. "Forcing them to come isn't the answer." He drew a fake flower from his vest pocket and showed the audience. "If you use some form of bribery, it might get them here—but will it keep them?" He shook his head. "I doubt it, and I don't think that's the way Jesus meant for us to preach the good news. We need to live the Christian life so others will see Jesus shining through us. Then, when we invite our friends and family to church, they'll want to come and see what's it all about." He shook his head slowly. "Shame on me for trying to make you think otherwise."

Joe held the flower in front of his own face and squeezed the attached bulb. A stream of water squirted on his nose, and the audience clapped heartily. Joe took a bow and dashed out of the room.

Joe didn't wish to disturb the church service, so he stayed in the small room outside the sanctuary, listening to the pastor's message from his seat near the door. After the congregation was dismissed, Joe stepped over to the pastor. "If you're not too busy, may I speak with you for a few minutes?"

"Sure, Joe. I have time to talk now."

Joe followed Pastor Cummings down the hall to his office where they sat down in easy chairs.

The pastor leaned forward. "You're an excellent clown, Joe. God's given you a special talent, and it's good to see you using it for Him."

Joe folded his arms. "If I can bring a smile to someone's heart, it's a ministry worth doing."

Pastor Cummings nodded. "Most people seem to open up to a clown. I've noticed that the barriers seem to come down the minute you step into a room."

"You're right, but I've seen a few exceptions," Joe said. "I remember being in a restaurant one time to do a kid's birthday party, and an older man was sitting at a nearby table. He seemed nervous by my presence and stayed hidden behind his newspaper until I left."

"Guess he forgot what it was like to be a child."

Joe shrugged. "Could be."

Pastor Cummings wrinkled his forehead. "Maybe the man was afraid to laugh. Some people have a hard time getting in touch with their emotions—especially if they've been hindered during their growing-up years."

Joe shifted uneasily in his chair. Could the pastor see inside his heart and know how discouraged he'd been as a child? Did he know how hard it was for him to get in touch with his feelings?

"What did you wish to speak with me about, Joe?"

Joe's nerves were as taut as a rubber band. This was going to be harder than he thought. "I'm. . .dating a woman now who is. . .well, Lois tends to be kind of serious."

"Does that bother you?" the pastor asked.

"Not really, because she's recently taken a couple of clowning classes and is learning to relax and joke around."

"Then what's the problem?"

"I think I'm the problem," Joe said.

"How so?"

"Lois wants to know about my family and what went on in my past."

"And I take it you'd rather not talk about that part of your life?"

Joe nodded. "The truth is, I don't even want to think about the past, much less discuss it."

He took a few deep breaths and tried to relax. The only sound was the soft ticking of the clock on the wall behind the pastor's desk.

Suddenly an image of Joe's mother popped into his mind. He could see her shaking her finger at him. He could hear her shouting, "You're a slob, Joseph Andrew Richey! Why can't you do anything right?" She slapped his face, then ran from his room, sobbing and shouting obscenities.

"Why was she always so critical?" Joe mumbled to himself. "Why was everything I did never good enough?" His voice lowered even more. "Why couldn't she at least say something positive about me?"

"Who was critical of you, Joe?"

Joe raised his head. Pastor Cummings was staring at him. "Oh. I guess I was sort of daydreaming. All of a sudden I could see my mother and hear her shouting at me."

"Both of your parents are dead, as I recall from what you told me when you first started coming here. Is that right?" the pastor asked.

Joe nodded.

"Were you and your mother close?'

"I–I guess so. I did everything she asked, even when she wouldn't take her medicine and sort of flipped out."

"Was your mother ill?"

Joe swallowed past the lump wedged in his throat. How could he explain about Mom? Would Pastor Cummings understand, or would he be judgmental, the way Joe's childhood friends had been when they'd seen his mother in one of her moods?

"Being able to talk about your feelings will help you get in touch with them," the pastor prompted.

"My mother was mentally ill," Joe blurted out. "She was diagnosed with manic depression, but she never acknowledged it or took the medicine the doctor prescribed."

"I see. And how did her illness affect you, Joe?"

Joe stood suddenly. "I've spent the last week alone, wrestling with my past, and I thought I was ready to talk about it—but now I don't think I am."

The older man nodded. "It's okay. We can talk more when you're ready."

Joe was almost to the door when he felt the pastor's hand touch his shoulder.

"I want you to know, Joe, that I'm here for you. Anytime you need to talk, I'm available," Pastor Cummings said in a sincere tone.

Joe nodded and forced a smile on his face. "Thanks. I'll remember that."

twenty-one

Lois stared at the telephone, praying it would ring. If only she would hear from Joe. It had been two weeks, and she was getting more worried. She was reaching for the phone when it rang.

Startled, she grabbed the receiver. "Hello."

"Hi, Lois. It's Joe."

Lois felt as though the air had been squeezed from her lungs. She hadn't talked to Joe since Thanksgiving and had almost given up hope of ever hearing from him again.

"Are you still there, Lois?"

"Yes, I'm here."

"How have you been?"

"Fine. And you?" Lois knew they were making small talk, but she didn't know what else to say. Things seemed strained between them.

"Well, the reason I'm calling is, I was wondering if you're still mad at me."

"I was never mad, Joe."

"Okay. Irritated then."

"Not even that. I was a bit disappointed because you left so abruptly on Thanksgiving and wouldn't tell me what was bothering you."

"I'm sorry, but my brother had me pretty upset," Joe said. "I took off for Ocean Shores and stayed a whole week."

"An impromptu vacation?" Lois asked.

"I needed time to think. I've been doing a lot of that lately."

"What have you been thinking about?"

"You. Me. My past."

"Want to talk about it?"

"I'd like to talk about you and how you make me feel," he replied.

"Oh. How's that?"

Joe paused. Then in a high voice he sang, "Some might think I'm a clown who laughs and doesn't like to frown. But I'm really a lovesick fellow who's too scared to say so 'cause he's yellow."

Lois laughed, in spite of her confused feelings. "Did you make up that little ditty?"

"Guilty as charged."

Lois wondered if Joe really did love her. In a roundabout way he'd said he did, if his silly tune proved how he felt. She chuckled as she played the words of Joe's song over in her head.

"You're laughing at my love tune?" Joe asked.

"Not really. It's just—"

"I'll be the first to admit I can't carry a tune in a bucket."

Before she could reply, he asked another question. "Are you doing anything special for Christmas?"

Lois hesitated. Was he hinting at spending the holiday together, or was he trying to change the subject? "I'll be spending Christmas Eve with Tabby and Seth and his grandparents, at their retirement home. On Christmas Day we'll be in Olympia with Mom, Dad, and my grandmother."

"If you're coming to Olympia, why don't you stop by my house for awhile? You could make it either before or after your visit with your folks."

Lois considered Joe's offer then asked, "Don't you have any plans for Christmas?"

"Brian said he might stop by sometime on Christmas Eve, but other than that I'm on my own."

Lois's heart sank at the thought of Joe spending the holiday by himself. It wasn't right for anyone to be alone on Christmas Day. "Why don't you come over to my parents' place for Christmas dinner? They aren't Christians, but they're very hospitable, and I'm sure they'd enjoy meeting you."

"Will Seth and Tabby be there?"

"As far as I know."

Joe was silent for a moment, and then he chuckled.

"What's so funny?"

"Nothing. I'd like to join you for dinner. Just give me your parents' address, tell me what to bring, and I'll be there with my Christmas bells on."

&

Lois groped for her slippers and padded to the bedroom window. She had been hoping for a white Christmas, but the brilliant blue sky that greeted her on Christmas morning was filled with sunshine and fluffy white clouds. She studied the thermometer stuck to the outside of the glass. Ten degrees above freezing, so there was no snow on the horizon. At least it wasn't raining. Lois would be driving the freeway from Tacoma to Olympia on bare, dry roads, and for that she was thankful.

She had spent Christmas Eve in pleasant company with Tabby and Seth and his dear Christian grandparents. Today would be a sharp contrast. Although her grandmother had recently become a Christian, her parents still refused to see their need for the Lord. Lois hoped her light would shine so they could see how God had changed her life for the better.

Tabby and Seth felt the same way. And with Joe there for Christmas dinner, her parents would be surrounded by Christians. She hoped it would make a difference in their attitude toward spiritual things.

❧

Whistling "Jingle Bells," Joe sauntered up the sidewalk toward the Johnsons' brick home. He was in better spirits this Christmas than he had been in many years. Brian had come by his home the night before and told him he'd found a tract someone had left in his cab. He'd been civil and even said he was thinking about going to church. That was an answer to prayer, and if Brian did start attending church, maybe he would finally see his need for Christ. Joe had witnessed to his brother several times over the years, but Brian always refused to talk about it. Now Joe felt as if there might be hope. He would continue to pray for his younger brother and with God's help try to understand him and work toward a better relationship.

Joe glanced down at the Christmas present he'd brought for Lois. He was also carrying a box of cream-filled chocolates he planned to give her folks. He was eager to meet them and hoped they liked candy.

He hesitated a second then rang the bell. Almost at once Lois opened the front door, and the sight of her took his breath away. She was wearing a blue velvet dress that matched her eyes and almost reached to her ankles. Her hair hung down her back, held away from her face with two pearl combs. He thought she looked like an angel.

"Come in," Lois said, warming Joe's heart with her smile. The sparkle in her eyes told him she was glad to see him.

He handed her the wrapped package, along with the chocolates. "The gift's for you, and the candy is for your folks."

"That's so sweet. I have something under the tree for you too."

Joe followed Lois down the hall and into a cozy living room, where Seth and Tabby sat on the couch beside a middle-aged woman he assumed was Lois and Tabby's mother. She had brown hair and eyes like Tabby's, and her smile reminded him of Lois. Across the room sat an older woman with short, silver-gray hair and pale blue eyes. Lois's grandmother, he guessed. A man with thinning blond hair, a paunchy stomach and eyes the same color as Lois's was relaxing in a recliner near the fireplace. He stood when Joe entered the room. To complete the picture, a fir tree decorated with gold balls and white twinkle lights took up one corner of the room. Joe inhaled the woodsy scent and smiled. It was a pleasant scene, and he was glad he'd come.

"Mom, Dad, Grandma," Lois said with a sweep of her hand, "I'd like you to meet Joe Richey." She turned to Joe and smiled, then nodded toward the woman sitting beside Tabby. "This is my mother, Marsha Johnson."

Mrs. Johnson offered Joe a tentative smile. "Welcome, and Merry Christmas."

Lois gestured toward the older woman sitting in the rocking chair. "I'd like you to meet my grandma, Dottie Haskins."

Grandma Haskins winked at Joe. "It's so nice we're finally able to meet. We've heard a lot about you, young man."

Joe grinned when he noticed Lois was blushing. Apparently she'd been talking about him to her family. "Thanks. It's great to be here."

Lois's father came forward, his hand extended. "And I'm Earl Johnson." He scrutinized Joe a few seconds, then his face broke into a broad smile. "I understand you're a clown."

Joe nodded, reaching for his hand.

"I remember seeing some hilarious clown routines when I was a kid and went to the circus. Have you ever worked in a circus?"

"No, I'm a gospel clown, but I also do kids' birthday parties and some other events."

"Well, I'm pleased to meet you, Joe."

"Likewise, Mr. Johnson."

"Earl. Please call me Earl."

Joe pumped his hand. He liked Lois's dad. The man had a firm handshake, and he seemed taken with the idea that Joe was a clown.

"Look what Joe brought," Lois said, handing the box of chocolates to her mother.

Mrs. Johnson looked at Joe and smiled warmly. "Thank you. I'll pass the candy around after dinner so everyone can have some."

"Unless Tabby gets one of her pregnancy cravings and can't resist the temptation to dive into the box before then," Seth said with a deep chuckle. He winked at Joe and nudged his wife gently in the ribs.

"How would you like to sleep on the couch tonight?" Tabby asked, wrinkling her nose at Seth.

He held up one hand. "Not on Christmas Day. It wouldn't be right to kick a man out of his warm bed on Christmas."

Everyone laughed, and Joe took a seat on the floor in front of the fireplace. It felt good to be here with Lois and her family. It had been a year since he'd spent Christmas with anyone, and that had been just he and Mom.

Lois placed the gift Joe had given her under the tree and

dropped down beside him, settling against a couple of throw pillows. "Dinner should be ready soon, but if you're hungry we put some cut-up veggies and dip on the coffee table."

Joe glanced at the tray on the table, and his stomach rumbled. He was hungry, but he thought he'd better not fill up on munchies, since the real thing would be served soon.

Everyone engaged in small talk for awhile, then Mrs. Johnson stood up. "I'd better check on the turkey."

"Would you like some help, Mom?" Tabby asked.

"That's okay, Honey. You look kind of tired today, so stay put and rest."

Mrs. Johnson's gaze swung to her younger daughter, and immediately Lois stood to her feet. She looked down at Joe. "Keep the fire warm. I'll be back soon."

❧

Lois helped take the turkey out of the oven, then mashed the potatoes while her mom made gravy. She hoped everything was going okay in the living room. Joe appeared to be well received by her family and at ease with everyone.

"Dad seems to have taken a liking to your clown friend," her mother said.

Lois smiled. "Joe's an easy guy to like."

"Like or love?"

Lois's head came up at her mother's direct question. "Who said anything about love?" She searched for words that wouldn't be a lie. "Joe and I are good friends, and even though I care deeply for him, we do have a few problems."

Her mother stirred the gravy. "What kind of problems?"

"Joe's very reserved when it comes to talking about his past, and he doesn't show any emotion but laughter."

"But don't you think being around someone who looks at

the bright side of life would be better than having a friend who's full of doom and gloom?"

Lois nodded. "Yes, you're right about that. But too much laughter and clowning around could get to be annoying at times. It seems as if it would be better to have something in between, more of a balance, for a relationship to work."

"You have a point, Dear, but keep an open mind. A man can have much worse traits than being a funny guy."

"I know, Mom, and I'm trying to stay open-minded."

Her mother moved away from the stove and went to the sink. "This gravy is still a bit too thick. I'd better add more water to the flour mixture."

"I imagine you're looking forward to becoming a grand-mother in the spring," Lois said then.

Her mother groaned softly. "I'll say, but it's kind of scary to think about being a grandma. It's been a long time since I held a baby, much less changed diapers or tried my hand at burping."

Lois dropped butter into the potatoes. "It will come back to you." She chuckled. "It's probably like riding a bike. Once you learn, no matter how long it's been between rides, you still remember how to hold onto the handle bars and steer the silly thing."

"I hope you're right. I don't want to mess up my role of grandma as badly as I did mothering."

Lois whirled around to face her mother. "What are you talking about? You were a good mother. You always saw that our needs were met."

Her mother's eyes filled with tears. "I did my best to see to your material needs, but I'm afraid I failed miserably at meeting your emotional needs." She blinked several times.

"Especially Tabby's. I should never have let your father make fun of her the way he did."

Lois wiped her hands on a dish towel and hurried to her mother's side. She put her arms around her shoulders and hugged her. "I'm afraid Dad wasn't the only one guilty of tormenting Tabby. I did plenty of that myself."

"Another area where I failed," the older woman said tearfully. "I should have prevented it from happening. Instead, I watched you and your father become close while Tabby stood on the sidelines feeling insecure and ugly." She gave Lois's arm a gentle pat. "I'm glad the two of you have mended your fences. Even Dad and Tabby are getting along better these days." She stepped back then looked at Lois. "I. . .went to church with your grandmother last week. Did she tell you?"

Lois's mouth dropped open. "She never said a word, but I'm glad to hear it."

"We asked Dad to join us, but he wouldn't budge out of that recliner of his. He said a game was playing on TV, and he wasn't about to miss it."

Lois smiled to herself. She was so grateful her grandmother had made a commitment to the Lord, and now her mom had attended church. Hope for her dad, for both of her parents, welled up inside her.

ఌ

Joe sat at the Johnsons' dining room table, enjoying each bite of food he ate. Lois's mother was a good cook, and she also seemed quiet and steady. *Nothing like my mom,* he thought. Being around Lois's father was a pleasure for him too. Since his own dad died when he was young, he'd grown up without a father. *Maybe if Dad hadn't been killed, Mom would have been easier to live with. At least she'd have had a husband to lean on, and*

Dad might have persuaded her to take the medicine the doctor pre-scribed. Maybe if she'd become a Christian sooner—

"Lois mentioned you use balloon animals and some jug-gling in your clown routines."

Grandma Haskins's pleasant voice pulled Joe abruptly from his thoughts.

"Oh—yes, I do," he said, blinking.

"Maybe you could give us a demonstration after we've fin-ished dinner and opened our gifts," Lois's mother suggested.

Joe looked at her and smiled. "I suppose I could put on a little skit."

"When I was a boy I used to dream about running away from home and joining the circus," Lois's dad put in. "I either wanted to be a clown or a lion tamer." His stomach jiggled when he laughed.

Joe chuckled. "Now that's quite a contrast, Mr. Johnson—I mean, Earl. Did Lois tell you she's learned some clowning tricks?"

He felt an elbow connect to his ribs and knew Lois wasn't thrilled with his question.

"She's never mentioned it," her mother said, raising her eyebrows. "Lois, maybe you and Joe could perform a routine together, the way Tabby and Seth do."

"That would be fun to watch," Tabby agreed.

Joe glanced at Lois and saw her frown. He knew she wasn't happy about doing a clown routine with him. He reached for her hand under the table. "Lois has taken only a couple of clowning classes, and she's still practicing. Maybe it would be best if I went solo this time."

Lois let out her breath. "Joe's right—he will do much better without me."

twenty-two

During the rest of dinner, Joe remained quiet, answering questions only when they were directed to him. He was reviewing in his mind the clown routine he planned to do, as well as thinking about what he wanted to say to Lois before he went home.

After they finished eating and the table was cleared, everyone moved to the living room to open Christmas presents. Joe felt out of place, as each member of Lois's family exchanged gifts. Besides the candy, he'd brought only one gift, and that was for Lois. Joe had hoped to give it to her in private, but it didn't look as if that would happen.

"Only two presents are left," Tabby said, as she stacked the items she'd received onto the coffee table.

"One's mine to give Joe, and the other he brought for me," Lois said. She went to the tree and picked up Joe's gift. Joe followed, and they handed each other their presents.

"Should we open them at the same time or take turns?" Joe asked.

Lois shrugged. "Whatever you'd like to do is fine with me."

"Let's open them together," he suggested. "On the count of three. One—two—three!" Joe reached into the green gift bag and pulled out a necktie with a painting of Noah's ark and a rainbow on the front.

"Thanks, Lois. This is great," he said with sincerity.

"You're welcome." Lois tore the wrapping off her gift and

peered inside. Then she looked at Joe.

"What is it?" Tabby asked, craning her neck to see around Seth, who sat beside her on the couch.

Lois held up a bright orange construction worker's hat with a bunch of gizmos attached. Even to Joe it looked weird.

"What in the world is that?" Lois's father asked from his chair across the room.

"It looks like something from outer space," Seth said, laughing. "Why don't you model it for us, Lois?"

❧

Lois stared numbly at the so-called "hat" Joe had given her. Two empty cans of soda pop were attached to either side, each connected to a giant plastic straw that trailed over the top of the hat. A third straw came up the back then down over the bill. Hooked to one corner of the helmet was a microphone cord, which was attached to a small metal box with a red lever on the side. Lois had no idea what Joe expected her to do with it.

"I–I thought it would be a nice addition to your clown out-fit," Joe said, his face flushed. "Why don't you try it on and show us what it can do?"

Lois stood there, her gaze shifting from Joe to the grue-some hat and back again. She would never wear such a hideous thing! What had possessed the man to give her this ridiculous Christmas present? She handed the hat to Joe. "Here—you wear it."

He shrugged and set it on top of his head. "I might as well show you how it works while I do my clown routine."

Lois sat down on the couch beside Tabby, folded her arms across her chest, and watched.

Joe flicked the red button on the small box attached to the

microphone, and suddenly a high-pitched noise pierced the air.

Lois cupped both hands over her ears and grimaced. She noticed Mom and Grandma had done the same. Tabby, Seth, and Dad were all smiling as if Joe had done something great.

Joe switched the red lever to the right this time, and bells started ringing. He jumped up and down. "Are those Christmas bells, or is the fire alarm going off?" he shouted.

Before anyone could respond, he bent down and grabbed an orange and two apples from the glass bowl sitting on the coffee table. One at a time he tossed the pieces of fruit into the air, and he soon had them going up and down simultaneously.

Lois had to admit that Joe was good at juggling—and all other phases of clowning for that matter. In minutes he could captivate an audience, as he apparently had her family.

"What goes up must come down!" Joe shouted into the makeshift microphone. "Anyone thirsty?" He continued to juggle the fruit as he pretended to drink from the straw connected to the cans. As if that weren't enough of a show, Joe did it while he hopped on one foot.

Everyone cheered, and Lois noticed her father was laughing so hard tears were streaming down his cheeks. Joe's goofy antics had sure made an impression on him. If Slow-Joe the Clown comes around more often, Dad's interest in spiritual things might even be sparked.

As he juggled the fruit, Joe talked about Christianity and how people often juggle their routines to squeeze in time for God. When he was finished, he dropped the fruit back in the bowl, then bowed. Everyone clapped, including Lois. Joe had done a good job of presenting the good news, and he'd made her family laugh. Not only was Slow-Joe a great entertainer, but he was a lot of fun. Was that enough? she wondered.

❧

As the day wore on, Joe began to feel nervous. He liked Lois's family, and he had finally admitted to himself that he was in love with Lois. During the first part of the day she'd been warm and friendly, but since he'd given her that dumb hat and done his impromptu routine, she'd been aloof. He wondered if she were sorry she'd invited him today. It might be his first and last meal at the Johnsons' home, and in his book that would be a real shame.

When Lois excused herself to clear away the dessert dishes, Joe jumped up and followed. "Need some help?" he asked, stepping into the kitchen behind her.

Lois placed the pie plates in the sink. "You rinse, and I'll put the dishes in the dishwasher."

"I think I can handle that." Joe went to the sink and turned on the faucet. He waited for Lois to say something, but she remained quiet as he rinsed the plates and handed them to her.

When the last dish was in place and the dishwasher turned on, Joe reached for Lois's hand. "I had a good time today. Thanks for inviting me to share your Christmas."

She nodded. "You're welcome."

Joe leaned forward, cupped Lois's chin with his hand, and bent to kiss her.

She pulled away abruptly. "We should get back to the others."

"I blew it with that dumb gift I gave you, didn't I?"

She looked at Joe, tears gathering in her blue eyes. "You made a hit with my dad."

"But not you?"

She pressed her lips together.

The tears in Lois's eyes were almost Joe's undoing, and he was tempted to pull her into his arms and say something funny so she would laugh. He hated tears. They were for weak people who couldn't control their emotions.

"I'm in love with you, Lois," he whispered.

Lois stared at him, her eyes wide.

"Aren't you going to say something?" he asked, tipping her chin.

"I—I'm speechless."

Joe chuckled and kissed her forehead. When she didn't resist, his lips traveled down her nose and across her cheek then found her lips.

She wrapped her arms around his neck and returned his kiss. Finally, Lois pulled back and sighed, leaning her head against Joe's chest. "I love you too, but I think you might need a woman who's more like you."

Joe took a step backward. "What's that supposed to mean?"

She shook her head slowly. "You're a clown, Joe. You clown through the day and into the night."

"That's my job, and I hope I'm good at what I do."

"You are," she assured him.

"Is it because I don't make a lot of money clowning? Is that the problem?"

Lois shook her head. "I've told you before that I'm not hung up on money. But the thing is, all you ever do is clown around. You make jokes when other people would be saying something serious. You don't show any other emotion besides happiness. I suspect you do it to avoid revealing your true feelings." She paused. "After that scene with your brother on Thanksgiving, I think there's a lot you haven't wanted to share with me. I respect your privacy, Joe. But if we're going to continue our relationship, don't you think you need to trust me by sharing what happened in your past that has upset you so much?"

Joe looked at his feet. Lois was right; he needed to be up-front with her and stop hiding behind his clown mask to keep from facing his true feelings. But he wasn't sure he could do either yet. Maybe he needed a few more sessions with Pastor Cummings.

"I'm not ready to discuss my family's problems at the moment," he said, offering her what he hoped was a reassuring smile. "But if you'll be patient with me, I hope maybe someday. . . ."

She squeezed his hand. "Let's both be praying about this, okay?"

He nodded and brought Lois's fingers to his lips. "I'd better be going. It's been a great day, and no matter what happens down the road, always remember I love you."

twenty-three

Joe sat in the chair across from Pastor Cummings's desk, his left leg propped on top of his right knee. Today was his fourth counseling session, and each time he entered this office he became more uncomfortable. The pastor had a way of probing into Joe's subconscious, and some of the things he'd found there scared Joe.

"Tell me more about your mother," the older man said.

Joe released his breath and with it a deep moan. "Well, I've told you she was very depressed one minute and happy the next, and she only got worse after Dad was killed. Her moods were so unpredictable and her expectations ridiculous." He dug his fingers into the sides of the chair and fought against the urge to express his anger. "It was because of Mom's actions that Brian left home shortly after high school. She made our lives miserable when she was alive, but I still loved her."

"Of course you did, Joe." Pastor Cummings leaned forward, resting his elbows on the desk. "What did you do about your mother's actions?"

Joe shrugged his shoulders. "To avoid her anger, I gave in and let her have her way on things—even stuff I felt was wrong." He looked at the pastor. "It was easier than fighting back and suffering the consequences of her frequent outbursts."

"If I've been hearing you right, you felt as though your mother wanted something you weren't able to give."

Joe moved in the chair, putting both feet on the floor. "That's correct. Sometimes I just wanted to shout, 'Go away, Mom, and leave me alone!'"

"But you thought by your mother's actions that your feelings didn't matter?"

Joe nodded again.

"The truth is, they do matter. Because you didn't want to be like your mother, you've chosen to stuff your feelings down deep inside." Pastor Cummings picked up his Bible. "Part of the healing process is being able to accept the pain. God made our feelings, and He uses them to help guide us."

Joe only shrugged.

"Do you let yourself cry when you're hurting, Joe?"

Joe shook his head. "Tears are a sign of weakness. Mom was weak, and she cried a lot. Brian was weak, and he ran away from home." Joe pointed to himself. "I chose to stay and take care of Mom, even though she never showed any appreciation." He frowned. "When she was nice, I felt myself being drawn into her world, like a vacuum sucks lint from the carpet. When she was hateful, though, I wanted to hide my head in the sand and cry until no more tears would come. But I didn't."

"It's not a weakness to cry or hurt, Son. Tears can be a key element to strength."

Joe blinked. He'd never thought of tears being related to strength.

Pastor Cummings held the Bible out to Joe. "Here—open to Ecclesiastes, chapter three. Then read verses one to four."

It took a few seconds for Joe to locate Ecclesiastes. He read the passage aloud:

" 'To every thing there is a season, and a time to every purpose under the heaven. . . .A time to weep, and a time to laugh; a time to mourn, and a time to dance.'" He paused and looked at the pastor. "I guess I've never read those verses before, or if I have they never hit home."

"The Lord reveals the meaning of His Word when the need arises. Perhaps you weren't ready to accept the truth before today."

Joe swallowed hard. Pastor Cummings was right; he hadn't been ready. Even now, when he'd been hit with the truth, he was having a difficult time dealing with it. He'd spent so many years hiding behind his clown mask, refusing to show any emotion other than laughter, and even that was forced at times. He felt like a phony, realizing how often he'd clowned around or cracked jokes when deep inside he felt like weeping. Part of him wanted to give in to his tears. Another part was afraid if he did he might never stop crying.

"Mom asked the Lord to forgive her and committed her life to Him shortly before she died," Joe said. "Even though I knew God had forgiven her for treating me so badly, I guess I never forgave her." Joe lowered his head. "I've always felt guilty about it, so maybe that's part of the reason I've been hiding behind humor."

"You've discovered a lot in our last few sessions," the pastor said softly. "It will take time for you to put it into the proper perspective. For now, though, pat yourself on the back and rest in the Lord. He will show you how and when to cry if you need to."

Joe nodded, feeling as if his burden was much lighter than when he'd entered the pastor's study. Maybe someday he would even be ready to discuss his feelings with Lois.

⁂

The month of January and the first days of February drifted by like a feather floating in the breeze. Lois kept busy with her secretarial duties at the church during the week, and she spent most weekends helping Tabby redecorate their guest room, turning it into a nursery for the soon-coming baby. It kept her hands busy and her mind off Joe Richey. Since they'd said good-bye on Christmas Day, she'd heard from him only twice. Once he'd called to tell her how much he liked the cute tie she'd given him, and today she'd received a Valentine's card from him in the mail.

"Hey, Sis. You look as if you're a thousand miles away."

Tabby's sweet voice pulled Lois out of her musings, and she swivelled her chair around to face her sister.

"You're good at sneaking up on me," Lois said with a grin.

Tabby ambled across the room and lowered herself into the chair beside Lois's desk. She patted her stomach. "I'm practicing for motherhood. Aren't moms supposed to be good at sneaking up on their children and catching them red-handed?"

Lois chuckled. "You're right, but I was only typing a memo for Pastor Hanson. So you didn't catch me with any red color on my hands," she added, smiling.

"It looked more like you were daydreaming to me," Tabby said in a teasing tone. "Unless you've learned how to make that computer keyboard work without touching the keys."

"I guess I *was* caught red-handed," Lois admitted with a sigh.

"What, or shall I say whom, were you thinking about?"

Lois handed the Valentine to her sister. "This came in today's mail."

Tabby's eyes opened wide as she read the verse inside the card. "Sounds like the guy's got it bad, and it's a far cry from the funny clown hat he gave you for Christmas."

Lois lifted her gaze to the ceiling. "Sure—that's why he never calls or comes around anymore."

"Maybe he's been busy with performances. Entertaining is what he does for a living, you know." With her finger, Tabby traced the outline of the red heart on the card. "This Valentine could be a foreshadow of something to come, you know."

Lois was silent then finally said, "Yes, it could be."

Tabby stepped over to Lois's chair. "There are only two ways to handle a man." She laughed. "Since nobody knows what either of them is, I suggest you give the guy a call and thank him for the beautiful card."

"I'll think about it," Lois murmured. "But I've called him a lot over the last few months, and I don't want to seem pushy."

Tabby hugged her sister. "There's nothing pushy about a thank-you."

"True." Lois smiled. "Okay, I'll call him tonight."

"Good for you." Tabby started toward the door. "I need to get back to the day care. I've taken a longer break than I'd planned." She stopped suddenly and sniffed the air. "Say! Do you smell something?"

Lois drew in a breath. "Smoke. It smells like there's a fire somewhere in the building!"

twenty-four

Joe had battled the desire to see Lois for several weeks. But today was Valentine's Day, and he'd decided to take action. She would no doubt have received his card by now, so he hoped the sentimental verse might pave the way.

As he headed toward Tacoma on the freeway, all he could think about was the need to make things right with Lois. Through counseling with Pastor Cummings and studying the Scriptures, he'd finally forgiven his mother and come to grips with his past. Now he wanted to share everything with Lois. He hoped she would be receptive.

A short while later, Joe drove down the street toward Lois's church. His heart lurched when he saw two fire trucks parked in front of the building. As he pulled his pickup to the curb, he could see firemen scurrying about with hoses and other pieces of equipment. Billows of acrid smoke poured from the church.

Joe sprinted from his truck across the lawn, only to be stopped by a fireman. "You can't go in there, Sir. A fire started in the janitor's closet, and it's spread throughout most of the building."

"My girlfriend—she works here," Joe said between breaths. He would do anything to find Lois. "I have to get inside!"

The fireman put his hand on Joe's arm. "It's not safe. We're doing everything possible to put the fire out, so please stay out of the way."

Joe dashed to the back of the church, thinking he could slip in that door unnoticed. He had to find Lois and see if she was all right. Others might also be trapped in the church.

He had almost reached the door when two firemen stepped between him and the building. "Where do you think you're going?" one of the men asked.

"I need to get inside. My girlfriend—"

"Oh, no, you don't!" the other fireman shouted. "There's been a lot of damage to the structure. Most of the fire is out, but it's not safe in there."

Joe looked around helplessly, wondering if he could get inside another way. "What about the people inside?" he asked, feeling his sense of panic taking control.

He filled his lungs with air and prayed. *Dear Lord, please let Lois and everyone else be okay.*

Joe felt someone touch his arm. "I thought I saw your truck parked out front. What are you doing here?"

He spun around at the sound of Lois's voice, and the sight of her caused tears to flood Joe's eyes. His stomach knotted as he fought to hold back the tide of emotions threatening to wash over him. He didn't want to cry, but the tears came anyway. He was so relieved to see that Lois wasn't inside the church and appeared to be okay. "Thank God you're not hurt!" he exclaimed.

She smiled at him and reached up to wipe away the tears that had fallen onto his cheeks. "Joe, you're crying."

He nodded and grinned at her. "Yeah, I guess I am." He grabbed Lois around the waist and lifted her up, whirling them both around. "Thank You, Lord!" he shouted. "Thank You a thousand times over!"

"Put me down, you silly man! I'm getting dizzy," Lois said breathlessly.

Joe set her on the ground then placed both hands on her shoulders and stared into the depths of her indigo eyes. "Are you really all right, and did they get everyone out in time?"

She nodded, and her eyes pooled with tears. "Everyone is fine, but the building isn't. I'm afraid what's left of it may have to be torn down."

"The church can be rebuilt," Joe said, "but human life is not replaceable."

"You're so right," Lois agreed. "When the fire broke out, Tabby and I were in my office. Our first thought was about the day care kids who were in the basement."

Joe felt immediate concern. "Were they hurt?"

She shook her head. "Not a single child. Almost everyone was out of the building before the fire trucks even arrived."

"When I got here and saw all the commotion, then looked around and didn't see you, I was afraid you were trapped inside the church," Joe said, feeling as if he might cry again.

Lois smiled up at him. "It's nice to know you care so much."

Joe clasped her hand and gave it a gentle squeeze. "Thanks to my pastor's wise counsel and God's Word, I'm learning to put the past behind and show my emotions. That's why I drove over here, Lois. I wanted to tell you about it." He pulled a bunch of balloons from his jacket pocket and held them up. "I also wanted to give you these."

She tipped her head to one side. "Some deflated balloons?"

He chuckled and wiped his sweaty palms on the side of his blue jeans. "Well, I'd planned to show up at your office with a bouquet of balloon flowers—like the ones I made you the night we first met." Joe cleared his throat. "I, well, I came here to ask you a question."

"What question?"

Joe felt jittery all of a sudden. If he weren't careful, he would slip into the old Joe—the clown who didn't know how to show his real feelings.

He stuffed all but one balloon back in his pocket then blew up that one and twisted it into a wiener dog. He handed the pooch to Lois, bowed low at the waist and said, "Lois Johnson, will you be my housewife—I mean, maid—I mean—"

Lois stepped away, a puzzled look on her face. "You're such a big kidder, Joe."

⋅❧⋅

Joe watched Lois walk next door to the senior pastor's house. She'd thought he was clowning around when he tried to propose, and now she was probably mad at him.

Tears welled up in his eyes at the thought of losing her. He had meant for the proposal to be sweet and tender, and he'd botched it up but good, giving her a balloon dog then asking her to be his housewife. "What a jerk she must think I am," Joe mumbled, staring down at his feet. "What can I do now?"

"Go after her," he heard a voice whisper behind him. He turned to find Tabby standing near him. "Tell her you weren't kidding but just got nervous and messed up your presentation."

"Yeah, I guess you're right. I hope she'll believe me."

Tabby patted Joe on the back and started across the lawn toward the parsonage.

Joe sucked in a breath and offered up a quick prayer. Tabby was right; he did need to do something—quickly.

⋅❧⋅

Lois couldn't believe Joe was crying one minute, telling her he'd been in counseling and was learning to express his feelings, and the next minute he was joking about something as solemn as marriage. In light of the seriousness of the church fire, he was probably just trying to get her to chuckle. She shouldn't have been so sensitive. She wished she hadn't walked away so abruptly without letting him explain.

Tabby had entered the parsonage a few minutes earlier and gone inside with the others. Rather than talking about the fire with everyone, Lois was sitting on the front porch, trying to sort things out. She closed her eyes and was about to pray when she heard a familiar voice.

"Lois, I need to talk to you."

She opened her eyes as Joe took a seat beside her. He was smiling, but she saw the tension in his jaw. His smile seemed fake, like the one he painted on when he dressed as a clown.

He leaned closer, his face inches from hers, and Lois let out a sigh.

"I'm sorry about the dumb proposal and balloon dog," he murmured. "Would you take a walk with me so we can talk?"

She hesitated for a moment, uncertain what to say.

Joe grabbed Lois's hand and pulled her gently to a standing position.

She looked up at him. "What's going on?"

"I'm taking you someplace special."

Lois was tempted to resist. She couldn't explain the funny feeling she got every time she saw Joe. At some moments, like now, she had to fight the urge to throw herself into his arms.

They left the pastor's yard and walked in silence, until the small chapel behind the church came into view. It was used for intimate weddings, baptisms, and foot washing. "At least this building didn't catch on fire," Lois said as Joe opened the door and led her inside.

Joe nodded and motioned her to take a seat on the front pew. Then he knelt on one knee in front of her.

She squirmed uneasily and held her breath. What was he up to now?

"I love you, Lois," he whispered. "I know I'm not the ideal catch, and I'll probably never make a lot of money, but if you'll have me as your husband, I promise to love you for the rest of my life. Will you please marry me?"

Lois's vision clouded with tears as she smiled at Joe. "Yes. A thousand times, yes!"

His face broke into a huge grin. "Can I take that as a yes?"

She chuckled and winked at him. "It's a definite yes."

Joe stood and helped Lois to her feet then pulled her into his arms. "From now on we can clown around together, but I promise to get serious sometimes too."

She laid her head against his chest and sighed contentedly. "I'd like that, Joe. I want to spend the rest of my life telling others about God's love, and I want to be the kind of wife who loves you no matter how much you clown around."

A Letter To Our Readers

Dear Reader:

In order that we might better contribute to your reading enjoyment, we would appreciate your taking a few minutes to respond to the following questions. We welcome your comments and read each form and letter we receive. When completed, please return to the following:

Fiction Editor
Heartsong Presents
PO Box 719
Uhrichsville, Ohio 44683

1. Did you enjoy reading *Clowning Around* by Wanda E. Brunstetter?
   ❏ Very much! I would like to see more books by this author!
   ❏ Moderately. I would have enjoyed it more if

   _____

   _____

   _____

2. Are you a member of **Heartsong Presents**? ❏ Yes ❏ No
   If no, where did you purchase this book? _____

   _____

3. How would you rate, on a scale from 1 (poor) to 5 (superior), the cover design? _____

4. On a scale from 1 (poor) to 10 (superior), please rate the following elements.

   ____ Heroine   ____ Plot
   ____ Hero   ____ Inspirational theme
   ____ Setting   ____ Secondary characters

5. These characters were special because?_____
_____
_____

6. How has this book inspired your life?_____
_____
_____

7. What settings would you like to see covered in future
   Heartsong Presents books? _____
_____
_____

8. What are some inspirational themes you would like to see
   treated in future books? _____
_____
_____

9. Would you be interested in reading other **Heartsong
   Presents** titles? ❏ Yes   ❏ No

10. Please check your age range:
   ❏ Under 18   ❏ 18-24
   ❏ 25-34   ❏ 35-45
   ❏ 46-55   ❏ Over 55

Name_____
Occupation_____
Address_____
City_____ State_____ Zip_____

Heart♥ong

Any 12 Heartsong Presents titles for only $30.00*

CONTEMPORARY ROMANCE IS CHEAPER BY THE DOZEN!

Buy any assortment of twelve *Heartsong Presents* titles and save 25% off of the already discounted price of $3.25 each!

*plus $2.00 shipping and handling per order and sales tax where applicable.

HEARTSONG PRESENTS TITLES AVAILABLE NOW: